THE OPUS CAFÉ

Where the Lost are Found

A NOVEL

Book 3 – Opus Series

C. R. FRIGARD

Treebones Inc

Praise for *The Girl in the Yellow Scarf* –
Opus Series Book One

"A **candid** narrative of redemptive love, the heartwarming story of *The Girl in the Yellow Scarf*, although causing some tears, made for great discussion."
– *Lake Minnetonka Book Club Review*

AMAZON, GOODREADS & KIRKUS REVIEW

"A **heartwarming** story with finely drawn characters."
– *Tim Pickstone*

"Lots of smiles, good **chuckles** and my share of tears."
– *Karen Walshe*

"This is an **endearing** story of two people coming together through their love of music."
– *Laurie Harper*

"The author **captures** the essence of the change that takes place in a person when you add goodness and love to their life."
– *Melanie Caulfield*

"The **music** sang out from the pages, beautifully described."
– *Sharlene Boerema*

"A story of strong willed people who follow their **dreams**."
– *Karen Brooks*

"It is sweet and **riveting**."
– *Merrelyn Brand*

"Sentimental…**absorbing**…the pieces falling into place for Mike's opus are satisfying."
– *Kirkus Reviews*

Treebones Inc.
The Opus Café – Book 3 – Opus Series
C. R. Frigard

Editor: Pamela Illies
Cover and Interior Design: Peter Wocken

Published in the United States by Treebones Inc.
ISBN: 9781076157829

Scripture quotations are taken from the *Holy Bible*, King James Version.

First edition
Printed by CreateSpace,
a DBA of On-Demand Publishing, LLC

BOOKS BY C.R. FRIGARD

NONFICTION

Funthink: 12 Tools for Creative Problem Solving

Arthink: Creativity Skills for 21st Century Careers

FICTION

The Girl in the Yellow Scarf – Book 1 – Opus Series
Spring 2018

The Piano Man – Book 2 – Opus Series
Fall 2018

The Opus Café – Book 3 – Opus Series
Summer 2019

For my family

"I will seek that which is lost,..."
- Ezekiel 34:16

- Cast of Main Characters -

Mike Monroe – Musician/composer & mentor to *La Familia de Musica* Band
Naomi Williams – Musician/teacher & fiancée of Mike
Noah – African orphan
Rose Monroe – Family matriarch
Persis Monroe/Peterson – Older Sister to Mike/Married to Jesse Peterson
Trina (Runt) Monroe – Kid sister to Mike/student at Cornell
Jesse Peterson – Writer/Mike's friend & married to Persis
Reverend Robinson – Engaged to Mike's mother Rose
Reggie (R.G.) Green – Blind sax player
Rudy – Ex-cop/owner of Johnny's
Liz Shepard – Actress/former girlfriend of Mike
Professor Williams – Naomi's father
Marcus – Associate of Professor Williams

- *La Familia de Musica* – Band -

Jaz Jackson – Saxophone
Blake Richards – Piano
Abby Morrison – Violin
Mia Ma – Cello
Travis Grant – Brass
Cobi Morelli – Drums
Carlos Lopez – Bass guitar
Tobias Brown – Lead guitar

Mike Monroe, composer of the Broadway hit "The Girl in the Yellow Scarf" takes a sabbatical, leaving Leon Kohn, producer of "The Girl", puzzled. "We had everything lined up for another hit when Mr. Monroe bailed on me..." Seems unlikely Mike will find backing any time soon. But we'll miss his music.
Variety Magazine – July 1982

1

Surprise – Monrovia, Liberia, August 1982

Mike Monroe stood squinting out the passenger door of the Boeing 747 at what he could see of the tropical rainforest on the hills around Monrovia – heat pouring up from the steaming tarmac. *How do people breathe here?* His right leg was still bandaged and stiff from a gunshot wound just days before he left New York. A crazed junkie had shot him when Mike tried to break up a confrontation in the home of one of his music students. He still suffered night sweats from it but was thankful no one else had been shot.

"It must be a hundred and fifty degrees," Mike said, starting down the boarding ramp, a crutch under one arm and his fiancée, Naomi, holding onto his other arm. Rivulets of sweat already streamed down his temples.

"Oh, you'll get used to it. Just think of walking up 23rd Street in Manhattan with the wind chill below zero," Naomi said. She gave him a little squeeze as she smiled up at him – not a bead of sweat anywhere.

Mike had decided he couldn't take a chance of losing another person he loved. So, when it became obvious he and Naomi where meant for each other, he chose to follow her so she could honor a commitment to her father and help set up a school for orphans outside the capital of Monrovia. But he wasn't even sure what his role would be. And he was already missing the kids he mentored at the YMCA as well as performing in New York's top music venues. *Maybe I should've stayed and just waited for her to return?*

"I wish there had been time to tell my father you were coming," Naomi said. "But he should be happy there'll be two of us to help with the school."

Mike often relied on his gut and felt to his core he needed to come with Naomi. But her father, a professor at the university, remained a mystery. The few times he met him it seemed he had a wall around him and operated on a set of standards unknowable to Mike. In a word – he was strange.

As they crossed the tarmac to Customs, Mike was feeling more and more uneasy.

"In America it's customary to ask the father's permission to marry his daughter." Mike stopped and pulled her aside so the other passengers could pass. "I feel bad I didn't have that chance. It's a little late now."

Naomi reached for his face and held his gaze. "Mike, please relax. We're going to be fine."

Mike pushed on a smile, nodded and they turned for the terminal. After Customs, Naomi led Mike through the crowded airport looking for her father.

"Maybe he'll meet us in baggage claim," she said.

"Maybe he saw me and left."

"Stop it Mike. We landed on time. He's here somewhere."

After they retrieved their bags, they started for the exit – Naomi visibly getting agitated.

As they passed through the door outside, a young man ran up and stopped in front of Naomi, smiling broadly.

"Naomi?"

Naomi stepped back and peered askance at him. "Yes."

"Sorry, I'm late," he said, catching his breath as he reached for her bag – ignoring Mike. "I'm here to take you to your father."

Naomi wouldn't let go of her bag and yanked it back. "Who are you?"

"I'm Marcus," the handsome Liberian said. "I'm your guide…I guess. Your father said I was to look after you while you're here."

Mike stepped around the man and slid in between him and Naomi. "I think you might be assuming something. I'm here with Naomi and I will look after her while she's here."

Marcus shuffled back with a sneer, looking down at Mike. "Who are you?"

"I'm Mike Monroe, soon to be married to Naomi," Mike said, tightening his grip on his crutch.

Marcus had about four inches over him along with twenty to thirty pounds and didn't seem the least impressed with Mike.

"You have to be kidding," Marcus said with a snort. He looked past Mike to Naomi. "I think your father has other plans."

Great…really can't wait to meet the professor now, Mike thought.

2

Jaz – Manhattan, August

Jaz Jackson, one of Mike Monroe's music students from the YMCA, knocked and stood at the door of Mike's old flat on Bleecker Street – not sure what to expect. A week after Mike left for Africa she finally got around to checking in with R.G., the storied blind sax player from Mike's band, *The Gathering*, who had promised to mentor and help her find work while Mike was in Africa.

"Hey," she said when R.G. poked his head out.

"Ah, Jaz. Come in," he said, shuffling back with the door. "What's on your mind, girl?"

"Just check'n in on ya." She walked past R.G. and ambled to the ebony grand piano that took up the center of the studio apartment, sat down and plunked a couple keys.

"Maybe I should learn to play this thing."

"Why would you want to do that?" R. G. asked, closing the door and heading to sit at the old chrome and Formica table in the kitchenette.

"Who's gonna hire a solo sax player?"

"Tell me about it," R.G. said, leaning back after sitting down. "But there's always the subway or Washington Park."

Jaz groaned. "Yeah, there's that. What was your best day on the street?"

R.G. broke out a grin. "I'll never forget, one hundred thirteen dollars and sixty-five cents. Only because a Wall Street type dropped a C note in my case after getting a huge bonus. Maybe you should get you a white cane."

Jaz would never be the same after playing at the Radio City youth competition. Noted musician and composer Mike Monroe had formed the band of top young talent from all around New York. After working together for three months, they had jelled and could play just about anything. But, after the competition, Mike left for Africa with his fiancée to open a school for orphans. Everyone from the group was left to find their own way. R.G? Moved into Mike's apartment. And Jaz? Felt like an orphan herself.

Jaz got up from the piano and wandered over to the window. "Ever want to give it up, R.G.?" she asked, looking down at the bustle on Bleecker Street.

R.G. turned toward her voice. "What'd ya mean by that, Jaz?"

She shrugged and turned away from the window. "I don't know. I've got nothing. My dad, the junkie, is dead and Mr. M…probably gone for good."

R.G. grunted. "Get over here and sit down."

Jaz sauntered over and flopped onto the kitchen chair across from him.

"I don't want to hear 'bout givin' it up. Listen to me! You have a God given gift, designed special for you. You have a responsibility to use it proper like."

Jaz scowled like a scolded child.

"Sounds to me like you're feeling sorry for yourself," he continued. "You have this great talent and it doesn't seem enough for you."

Jaz sunk at the table while R.G. went on about his life. How he barely survived a beating in the civil rights movement in the 60's. How his mother died giving birth to his sister who he hasn't seen in twenty years. He never knew his father and he had been living on his own since he was twelve. He went blind from glaucoma when he was thirty-two and had nothing but a saxophone to make a living.

"Have I ever felt like giving up? Hell no!" R.G. smacked the table with his hand, causing Jaz to jump.

"You listen to me." He leaned over toward her. "Decide how you're goin' to use that gift of yours and get on with it." He settled back in his chair glowering.

Jaz swore she felt heat coming off his face – his dark glasses glaring above his tightly drawn lips. *Don't need an ol' black man yelling at me.*

Jaz sprang up and marched to the door. "I'm outta here, old man." She stopped and looked back. "Blake thinks he might have some work. Can't imagine anything worthwhile though."

"Jaz –"

Jaz pulled the door closed before R.G. could finish and cussed all the way down the four flights of stairs to the street. Now all she had to look forward to was how wonderful Blake's life was going. She needed to come up with something to top him. *Hell, I've got it made.* Then she laughed at the thought. Her poor mother was still healing from a beating by her father who, after shooting her beloved mentor, was killed by a car when he tried to escape the scene. So now she's mostly alone. Only an old blind man to watch over her and how can he do that? He can't see a damn thing.

Blake Richards' life was all planned out: follow his Uncle Robert's steps to become a New York physician; marry his beautiful girlfriend, Abby; and move into the prestigious Upper West Side neighborhood near his loving parents. There was just one problem with this plan of predicable ease. Blake got a taste of what it's like to perform for an adoring audience of thousands.

Playing piano at the Radio City youth competition was just something to do the summer of '82, before going off to college. However, he experienced a life-changing joy after the eight-piece band of teenage musicians won first place. He was hooked.

When Mike Monroe left New York with his fiancée for Africa, Blake struggled with how to move forward with his music. Making things worse his girlfriend, Abby, left for Europe to live with her parents.

He was heartbroken and had to sort out his new career choice by himself. His parents, although not pleased, gave him a year to get the idea of being a musician out of his system. But, for now, the only thing Blake had going was playing at

Johnny's Piano Bar – a job Mike had arranged before he left for Liberia.

After Abby left for France, Blake convinced Jaz to join him at Johnny's along with Albert, a bass player friend of Abby's. Promising to help Blake after Mike left town, Rudy, a retired NYPD detective and owner of Johnny's, gave the new combo a week to prove themselves – though he didn't care much for Jaz's smart mouth.

Following the last set on the last night of their trial period, Jaz asked Blake if he knew *Summertime*.

"Of course," he said. "Key of A minor okay?"

"If that works for you," she said with her eyebrows arched.

Albert chuckled as Blake slowly shook his head. "I'll give you a couple measures for nothing, hot shot."

Blake nodded four beats to Albert then began the intro. But, instead of playing the sax, Jaz set her horn down, took the floor mic next to the piano and eased into singing an Ella Fitzgerald style rendition. Blake couldn't believe what he was hearing. Appearing stunned, Rudy stopped what he was doing behind the bar. The dozen or so customers went silent as the trio fell into a sultry Porgy and Bess groove.

Jaz seemed gripped in a sad reverie as she held the last note – a sprinkling of enthusiastic applause rose from the handful of customers. After placing the mic back in the stand, she told Blake when she was a kid she used to sing along with Ella's records that her dad loved– before he got strung out on drugs. For the first time, Blake sensed a crack in her tough shell and the softness in her face called to him. He wanted to stroke it and kiss her lips.

But then, catching his eye, she huffed and jerked back with a frown. "God, Blake…whatcha lookin' at?"

He lurched like he had been slapped and stammered, "That was...that was great." With his face getting hot he turned to Albert, trying to recover. "What do you think?"

"Unbelievable, man." Albert peered at Jaz. "Do you know more songs like that?"

Jaz seemed fully back to herself. "I don't think so. I play the sax, remember."

Rudy had strolled over from the bar by then and heard what she said to Albert.

He cleared his throat to get the trio's attention as he stood next to the piano. "You need to know something, Jaz." They all looked at him strangely, not having seen him out from behind the bar before. "Ella is my all-time favorite. No offense about your sax playing but, I insist you sing a few of Ella's numbers with each set if you're going to work here."

Jaz yanked her face away and glared across the room.

Rudy had little time for artistic temperament. "You have a problem with that?"

She studied the floor for a moment then straightened, sucked in a long breath between her teeth and turned back in the direction of Rudy but did not look at him.

"Guess not." She picked up her sax and muttered, "If you insist."

The three of them watched her close up her sax case and start for the door.

"Wait. I'll go with you!" Blake hollered. Jumping up he followed – wanting her to be safe as it was going on one AM.

She turned momentarily, looked at him incredulously and continued through the door, letting it slam behind her.

Rudy rolled his eyes and headed back to the bar. Albert started packing up and Blake slumped into a chair visualizing Jaz's momentary loveliness that had caused his heart to zing.

4

Naomi – Monrovia, Liberia, August

"**W**hy does your father hate me?" Mike asked, rolling up the bamboo shade to let in the brackish evening breeze. Although on the verge of collapse, the small four-room bungalow that would be their home after they got married did have a nice view of the beach and surf.

"It was hard for him to give up on Marcus. I don't know what he was thinking," Naomi said as she sidled up beside him to take in the view. Even though the palm trees in the yard were on the brink of toppling due to erosion of the beach, the boundless Atlantic conjured up sweet memories of playing in the surf as a child.

Mike turned to her. "What am I going to do here? It's been two weeks and I still don't know how I'm going to fit in."

She put her hands on his shoulders to calm him. "I know you are not used to slowing down but this is a chance to do that. Now take a deep breath." She waited.

"I'm serious! Take in a long deep breath…then give me a smile."

Mike sucked in air through his nose, his lips in a tight smile.

"Well that's a start," she whispered, then grabbed his face and planted a long passionate kiss on him and pulled back waiting for a real smile.

Mike snorted and gave her a broad grin. "You know what would really make me happy?"

"Hum. Let me guess. A piece of your mother's famous peach pie?"

"Yeah, that's it. When's the next plane to New York?" he said with a corner of his mouth jerked up.

"Fine…go." Naomi turned sharply and started for the door.

Mike reached for her arm and pulled her back for a warm embrace. She knew where this was leading. She leaned back to remind him her father was coming soon to pick her up when the professor walked in the back door, unannounced.

Seeing them her father scowled. "We need to get going. The meeting with the school board starts in a half hour."

"Is it okay if Mike comes?"

Her father looked away. "I suppose, but I don't know what he can do there."

Naomi shook her head and stepped up to her father. "We *are* getting married. So he is a part of my life now. Besides, he has a degree from Cornell and loves kids."

On the long flight to Monrovia they had discussed wedding plans. Anticipating her father's reaction, they decided it should be simple and as soon as possible. The whole thing seemed surreal – everything happened so fast. With only three days before leaving for Africa, Mike had gotten an engagement ring, a ticket to Monrovia and proposed to her at the celebration party for the YMCA kids. Now they had to figure out what to do next. She was determined to move ahead regardless of her father's objection to Mike.

Her father tried to stare her down as he peered over his glasses. But he was no match for Naomi.

"Let's go!" he said and spun around, stumbling slightly on the uneven floorboards as he made his way to the patched-up screen door.

Mike moaned as he peered over at her. She wanted to give him a smile but her blood was beginning to boil. She was about to call a cab and head with Mike to the airport, but sucked it up instead.

Driving to the meeting they passed the corrugated metal roofs of the shantytown, which appeared to have grown despite the promises of prosperity from the newly installed president. Her heart ached seeing the spreading poverty and shabbily dressed children playing amongst the rubble. It reminded her why she was there – to help make a difference.

She peered over at Mike who seemed in a dark mood as he peered out his side window. *He gave up everything for me.* She had to figure out how to make this work.

5

Blake – Johnny's, Manhattan, August

Blake was thankful he had a steady gig at the fabled piano bar in Gramercy Park – after what happened this morning. Walking in under the faded blue awning with the peeling white letters, he stopped just inside to take it in: the battered but resonate baby grand along the left wall with tables and chairs radiating out; the bar on the right a long slab of mahogany with brass rail, stools and full-length mirror with backlit glass shelving stacked with sparkling liquor bottles and glassware.

After a couple weeks of modest success at Johnny's, Blake got the bug to move away from his meddling parents. When he told them he wanted to try living on his own to pursue a career in music instead of medicine, they were devastated and, following a heated discussion, withdrew all financial support. Blake wasn't quite ready to be totally cut off but, after the big blowout, he packed a few things in a duffle and headed out the door – not knowing when he would see them again.

When he got to Johnny's at eight, Jaz was already there.

"What's with the bag? Leaving town?" She said in her usual snarky tone.

"In a way, I guess."

Jaz frowned, "What's goin' on, Blake?"

"I need to find a place to live."

Jaz looked like she was about to explode – her cheeks puffed out and her eyeballs bulged.

"What?…What did you do?"

"Told my parents I want to try it on my own for awhile and they helped me along by kicking me out – today. I wasn't quite ready, but here I am."

"My god Blake, now you're in the same boat I am. Think that's the funniest thing I've…ever…heard," she said doubling over, laughing like a lunatic.

Rudy scowled at them from behind the bar, then hollered "HEY" as he motioned for them to come over.

"Whoa." Jaz snickered and whispered, "We're being summoned by his Highness."

"Stop it, Jaz. Johnny's all I got going, so play nice."

The two ambled over and stood at the bar. Rudy glared at them. "You two want to keep working here?"

"Yes sir," Blake said, as Jaz turned away covering her mouth. Blake elbowed her, hard, to get her to straighten up. She punched him back with everything she had, which wasn't much with only ninety-eight pounds behind it.

Rudy just hung his head and rubbed his face then looked at them. "I did promise Mike I'd give you guys a shot, but you don't want to mess with me. If you want to keep working here you've got to act professional…GOT IT?"

Jaz seemed struck when Mike's name was mentioned. "Yes sir," she said, peering down at her feet.

"Good. Now give me some sweet Ella to get back in my good graces."

𝄞

Following the last set, Blake and Jaz stood under the faded awning to Johnny's hoping for a break in the drizzling rain.

"Where to now, preppie-boy?"

"Don't call me that!" Blake barked.

"Whoa there, tough guy," Jaz said, and then gave him a friendly nudge. "Really, what are you going to do now?"

"Not sure. I don't have much money and we don't get paid for a week."

"Welcome to my world," Jaz said, trying to suppress a snort.

"Any ideas? Now that I'm living in your world."

Jaz looked up over his shoulder in thought. "Well, there are several options. A cardboard box in the warehouse district or... there's probably still room under the Brooklyn Bridge or...we could check in with R.G. for the night in Mike's old flat."

"Really? That's all you got?"

"Sure as hell not takin' you to my mother's."

𝄞

Standing in front of R.G.'s door, Blake hesitated, really hating to bother the old musician at almost two in the morning.

6

School – Monrovia, August

Battered by yet another deluge, Mike and Naomi sat huddled in the rickety structure that was the temporary school building. They watched a foot wide river of rainwater seep in from beneath one wall and flow along a well-stained path on the floor to empty through the back wall.

"So, this is it?" Mike asked as he watched waves of wind driven rain lash at the windows facing the ocean.

"Thought you liked storms," Naomi said.

"I do, but…I don't know." Mike got up and wove through the scattered desks and chairs in the dimly lit room and stood at the window watching the palm and idigbo trees sway violently in the torrent.

Naomi's father finally accepted that Mike wasn't going away so agreed to a date for their wedding, which was now set for the first week of September. His mother Rose, of course, was ecstatic and would fly over for a long weekend with his sisters, Trina and Persis, and her husband Jesse. Unfortunately, Reverend Robinson, Rose's constant companion these days, had to stay in New York to be with his mother who had taken a turn for the worse. Mike had gradually come to terms with his mother getting married again– while he still suffered some guilt for not taking over the grocery business his father had started before he died. Thankfully, Persis had stepped up to manage the stores freeing Mike to pursue his music.

Naomi got up and walked next to him and put her head on his shoulder. "Sorry. I know this isn't what you expected but we'll make it work. Look what you accomplished in a smelly storage closet at the Y in New York. The kids loved practicing there."

Mike knew the room didn't matter. Making music could transcend just about anything. But the thought of his Y kids brought on a veil of regret. He wished he could be in two places at once – here with the love of his life, and back home with the often-maddening yet soulful verve of his Y kids. And, he had to admit, he missed playing – even at Johnny's, the hole in the wall piano bar.

"How am I ever going to keep a piano in tune in here?" he said. "Oh yea, why should I worry. I haven't got a piano."

"Stop it Mike. You know one's coming in a couple days." Naomi pulled back with a frown. "What's really going on? Are you worried about the wedding?"

He had a sudden urge to run out into the storm. "I'm lost here," he moaned.

Mike had relented to the living arrangements. Him at the beach house and Naomi staying with her father in town, but he hated being alone. He felt trapped and missed walking down the hall to Jesse's for a beer and volunteering with Al at the soup kitchen and the bustle of New York and going with Naomi for a slice of pizza at Gino's and –.

"Want to go back?"

"Sure, but not without you."

𝄞

The next two weeks were spent setting up the beach house that would become their home and cleaning out the dilapidated future school structure further down the beach. The new school with four classrooms and multipurpose room was planned to open the end of the year. Meanwhile, they had to patch the temporary classrooms as best they could to keep rain and bugs out until funds for the new building arrived. Naomi's father had negotiated a grant while he taught at Columbia University in New York.

To help Mike feel he was contributing, Naomi put him in charge of setting up his room for music, math and phys. ed. In the adjoining room she would teach reading, writing and life skills – which could have been labeled survival skills with all that these kids had to face. To start with they would be responsible for approximately 12 children ages 5-9. The first day of school would be in a week, the Monday after their Friday wedding.

When she walked in from her classroom, Naomi caught Mike sitting at his desk shaking his head side to side.

"What is it, Mike?"

He hadn't heard her come in and pinched his eyes tight in embarrassment.

"Sorry. I was just thinking about a proper honeymoon at a nice ocean front resort. We got the ocean but I wasn't planning on having twelve kids along."

This tickled Naomi and she couldn't hold back a snort. She walked over, pulled up a chair and sat next to him with her arm around him.

"Didn't you say you wanted lots of kids?"

"Yeah, but not all at once." Mike lifted his head to show Naomi he was smiling. "I'll be fine now that the piano is here. It's in pretty good shape despite the humidity."

"Wish we could move the date for the first day of school back but it was all planned before we arrived," she said. "The kids are counting on it and some aren't in very good shape, emotionally." Naomi leaned into him. "I think the best thing to do for now is just love them and show that education is important."

$$\text{\clef treble}$$

Slow down, is what Naomi had told me. What does that even mean. Slow down and do what?

7

R.G. - Greenwich Village, August

R.G. had promised Mike he'd watch over his band of misfits from the Y while he was gone but he didn't think it would involve full time babysitting two troubled teenagers. Having lived without family and on the fringe of society most his life, it was hard for him to relate to them. However, the last two weeks had pushed R.G. to the edge – leaving their stuff laying around for him to trip over and coming and going without a word. When Blake and Jaz where heading out for Johnny's, again, without even acknowledging him, he had had enough.

"Before you two run off," R.G. said, whapping his cane on the kitchen table, "we need to talk."

Blake looked back from the door, alarmed – Jaz with a scowl.

"Come here and sit down," R.G. demanded. "If you're going to use this as home base while you grow up, we need some rules."

Jaz sauntered over and flopped in the chair. Blake headed for the piano bench and sat down.

"Why do we need rules?" Jaz asked. "This isn't even your place."

R.G. wanted to grab and shake her but had learned to give his anger a couple beats before reacting.

"I never had kids, so might make a mistake now and then. But I did promise Mr. Monroe I would try to keep you from self-destructing." R.G. paused, thinking of what to say next. "I've seen it all, in my day. Being talented is only part of being successful."

With a snarky look that R.G. couldn't see but assumed, Jaz raised her hand like she was in class.

"At the end of the week we'll have enough money to find our own place. So…you won't have to worry 'bout us anymore."

R.G. swore under his breath. "Blake, what are you thinkin'? Your parents know you're movin' in with Jaz?"

"They kicked me out. So I don't have to answer to them, I guess."

R.G. realized he was loosing control and it scared him. He didn't want to disappoint Mike, but dealing with this was beyond him.

"So what's your plan? Move in together, make beautiful music and some unwanted kids?" As soon as it came out of his mouth he knew he went too far.

Jaz choked. "Don't you need to have sex to have a kid?"

R.G. scrunched his face and shook his head. Jaz got up and pulled Blake to the door.

"Do you even care what I think?" R.G. said, a last ditch effort at reasoning with them.

"Not really," Jaz said, and yanked Blake out the door, then stuck her head back in.

"Don't wait up Ol' man. We'll be late."

R.G. had to do something. Besides dealing with Jaz and Blake, he hasn't a clue what was happening with the other Y kids. He needed help.

$$\oint$$

"Hello, Rose. It's R.G." He sat with the phone, seething with frustration.

"Good to hear from you. How are you and what's going on with the kids?"

R.G. sat a moment thinking how to answer her. "I don't know, Rose. I'm not doing so well. Feel I'm lettin' Mike down. And now, Blake and Jaz are movin' in together."

Rose was silent. R.G waited.

"Don't beat yourself up. These kids are just figuring out how to become adults. They're going to make mistakes. We just need to be there for them and love them." Rose paused. "I feel bad I haven't at least connected with Jaz."

"I never had kids, Rose. Not sure how to do this."

"Seems we need to find out what's going on with them. How about we get them together somehow. We're heading to Monrovia in a few days for the wedding but, when we get back, we could have a party or something."

"I like it," R.G. said, without hesitation, desperate for any idea.

"Give me all the phone numbers and I'll set it up and get back with the time and date. We could call it a reunion. They should like that."

After passing along the info, he thanked Rose and hung up. Now to the clinic to check on why he woke up this morning with the taste of blood in his mouth.

8

Trouble – Monrovia, September

Providence Baptist Church, birthplace of the Liberian nation in the 1840's, was Naomi's church before she came to America. Because of the short notice and a full schedule for weekend weddings, the Friday before school started was the best they could do. The only thing Naomi insisted on was wearing traditional Liberian wedding clothes, which they had ordered the first week they arrived.

Mike insisted his family stay at the exquisite and expensive Ducor Palace Hotel overlooking all of Monrovia and the Atlantic Ocean. Naomi's father saw it as an unnecessary expense. Mike saw it as essential considering they wouldn't have a big wedding and reception with hundreds of guests like Persis and Jesse.

With so much to do before tomorrow's wedding, they divided the duties. Naomi looked after last minute preparations at the church and Mike headed to the airport. After picking up his family, he had the limo driver tour the city sites then drop them at the hotel. Mike explained they were to charge everything they needed, that he would take care of the bill at the end of their stay.

Mike played it cool and sat back in the limo to catch his kid sister's reaction when they drove up to the entrance of the luxury five star hotel.

"Whoa," Trina said, gaping at the modern eight-story hotel as they pulled up the circular drive lined with palm trees and flags from other African nations.

"Mike, isn't this a little extravagant?" His mother questioned.

"It's only for a couple days. I want you comfortable and safe." Mike paused and decided not to worry them with the growing unrest in the country. "I know you must be exhausted from your flight so, rest up a bit and we'll come back to have dinner here at 6:00."

Mike got out of the limo and led his mother and sisters to the lobby while the driver took care of the luggage.

As they were heading to check in, Jesse motioned he wanted a word with Mike. After they got their room keys at the front desk, Jesse told the women to go up to the rooms with the bellman and their luggage. He would be up shortly. Mother, whose intuition was always on high alert, gave Mike and Jesse *the look* as the elevator doors were closing.

Jesse directed Mike to seats in the expansive atrium overlooking the endless azure Atlantic.

Jesse, in thought, squinted at Mike. "From everything you've told me about Naomi's father he sounds really unhappy about something. Or is it everything?"

"First of all," Mike said, "I was a big surprise. Seems I'm in the way of his plans for the school. To say nothing of a tall muscle-bound Liberian he had picked out for Naomi."

"Marcus?"

"He keeps showing up as if checking to see if I'm still around."

"He does have a nice smile," Jesse said with a smirk. "But you could probably take him."

"Thanks for the vote of confidence...I think."

"Not to worry. Bet he can't even play chopsticks."

Mike snorted and turned to watch the smartly dressed people gathering in the lobby.

"How's it feel to be in the minority...my brother?" Mike said raising his eyebrows.

Jesse smiled. "Oh, about the same as sitting around your mother's table at Sunday dinner."

"Oh yeah. I keep forgetting you're different."

"Different's okay...isn't it?"

Mike nodded with a grin. "Love you man. You know...I thank God for you. Now with Naomi joining the family it's just you and me against all those women," Mike said, thrusting his fist in the air. "Solidarity, my brother."

"Amen, brother," Jesse said over his shoulder as he turned for the elevator. "How 'bout a beer after dinner?"

Mike gave him a thumbs-up then glanced across the lobby to see his future father-in-law chugging toward him like a locomotive up a steep grade, Marcus trailing behind.

$\oint$

After dinner with family, Mike returned to his tattered beach bungalow replaying the bizarre confrontation with Naomi's father and went straight to the ancient fridge for a beer. He needed to think and took it to sit on the porch, white curling waves and rumbling surf in front of him. He couldn't believe it. *Did the professor actually threaten me?*

$\oint$

Jesse showed up at Mike's door an hour later with a big grin, a six-pack and a brilliantly shined pair of shoes.

"Glad to see you've learned something from me," Mike said, attempting a grin as he let him in. Jesse had shown up in obscenely scuffed shoes at his wedding to Persis and, to save him from his sister's wrath, Mike had to quickly exchange shoes with him minutes before the ceremony.

Being Mike's best man, Jesse had stopped over in a sorry attempt at a bachelor party but ended up with Mike going through his options in dealing with the professor.

"Catch 22 comes to mind," Mike said, scrubbing his forehead with both hands. "Expose the professor's plan to Naomi or try to convince her I need to head back to New York with her. Either way he's going to use the money for the school to advance his political agenda."

Jesse sunk back in his chair. "How much time do you have?"

"He said he's risking his life by not leaving before the wedding tomorrow."

"Why did he want Naomi to come back if he wasn't going through with the school?"

"He wanted it all. His daughter back here with him and using the money, as he put it, 'to save his country from disaster'."

Jesse moaned and shook his head. "I don't get why he even told you all this?"

"He thought once Naomi was here she would go along with the plan to *save Liberia*. Now that I'm not going away he has to deal with me." Mike shuddered. "Tell you man, I think he's capable of anything to further his cause."

"What do you mean by…anything?"

"Let's say he made it clear he wouldn't be responsible if something happened to me."

"Shiiit." Jesse's mouth fell open.

"I have to figure out if he's just a bully who is trying a last ditch effort to scare me off or if he's for real."

"Why would he wait 'til the last minute to tell you all this?"

"He came across pretty desperate, like his plans had changed."

Jesse looked to the heavens. "To think all I had to worry about was scuffed shoes."

Mike hooted in spite of his misery. "Think we might need another six-pack."

𝄞

Still dark out, Mike woke to Naomi's soft voice and nudging. "Wake up...*please*."

Mike squinted up at her, pain slashed across her face.

"My god, Naomi. What is it?"

"Father hasn't come home. His bed's not slept in. There's no message or anything."

Several scenarios scrolled through his mind. Should he give some time to see if the professor will show? But after a few beats his gut sent a message he didn't want to acknowledge. He got up and ambled to the kitchen like he was going to make coffee. Naomi spun around and came up behind him. "Did you hear me? My father isn't anywhere to be found!" She grabbed Mike to face her.

"What? You know something...what is it?"

Mike had been in several tight spots growing up, some for being in the wrong and some just for being black. But this was out of his realm. He had learned the hard way to be forthright with Naomi so took her hand and led her to the wicker loveseat on the back porch – the waves rumbling in the background.

He tried his best to be kind as he laid out what her father had told him. How he was an agent for a group that hoped to lead Liberia toward a better future, using the funds from the school for their cause. Mike left out the oblique comment about his safety.

Naomi looked like she didn't recognize him. "What about the children who are coming to start school on Monday? And what about our wedding?"

♪

By morning Naomi had formulated a plan that was both pragmatic and brave. Mike intuited this needed to be her call as it was her country. After notifying the police about her father they would continue with the wedding as planned. On Monday they would start school as planned and carry on as best they could to see where it all led. He marveled at her strength and faith that things would turn out for the best.

Lord, how I love this girl, Mike thought gazing at Naomi with the morning sun golden on her smooth dark skin. As they sat holding hands with their plans solidified, Jesse silently appeared with two steaming cups of coffee.

He stood facing them, squinting into the sunrise. "Well, am I going to be the best man today or not?"

Mike wrinkled his nose looking up at him. "Of course. It's all about you, man. Wouldn't want to disappoint."

"Good…so do you want this coffee or not?"

♪

Mike heaved a sigh when he saw Naomi and his family come out of the hotel elevator before heading to the church. This wasn't at all how he thought this day would go, but held it together as best he could for his bride.

"Michael dear," his mother said reaching out to him like she hadn't seen him in years. Persis, Jesse and Trina came up and surrounded him for a group hug as Naomi held back a moment with her hand to her chest. Mike broke away and went to her.

"You're beautiful. I don't deserve you."

"I know. But let's do this before I change my mind," she said with a smile that slid slowly into quivering lips as she squeezed back tears.

"Sorry…Mike…" Naomi gasped.

"Shhh." Mike pulled her in close. "This is about us. Nothing else matters right now."

Mike wasn't too surprised when Naomi's father didn't show for the afternoon wedding and Naomi didn't seem to expect him either. He sensed she knew something was up but had kept it to herself.

9

Beginnings

When they first arrived in Monrovia Mike's attempt to follow Liberian tradition by offering kola nuts and a dowry to Naomi's father was squelched. The professor had scoffed, dismissing the matter with 'Don't worry about it Mike' and changed the subject as if nothing more needed to be discussed. Naomi was troubled when Mike told her about it, turning away in silence. From then on she had avoided her father and clung to Mike whenever they were around him.

A dozen distant relatives had shown up for the wedding ceremony with an uncle standing in for Naomi's absent father. The reception was held on a patio adjoining the back of the church with traditional Liberian food served: baked fish, fu fu (made from cassava), potato greens and palm wine. However, Rose did manage to have a wedding cake delivered from the Ducar Hotel – causing Naomi's eyes to glaze with tears along with an appreciative smile.

Mike's family encircled the newlyweds with smiles and pleasant conversation up to the time they needed to leave on Sunday. After a tearful farewell at the airport, Mike insisted on a "last supper" with Naomi at the Ducor roof top restaurant before school started the next day.

After their meal, Mike got up to talk with the maître d' then strolled to the baby grand piano in the middle of the room and beamed at Naomi while he played one of her favorites; *Somewhere Over The Rainbow*. The table chatter hushed throughout the room as Mike tenderly rendered the classic, causing tears of joy to slide down Naomi's cheeks. Mike was hardly aware of the applause when Naomi came over to kiss him and slide in next to him on the bench. Then for the next half-hour they sang to each other as if no one else was in the room. With a crowd gathered around the piano Mike looked up as if woken from a dream.

"Oh, sorry," he said. "Got carried away, I guess." A little embarrassed, they got up and returned to their table.

"I don't know about you but that felt good," Mike said as they sat down.

Naomi looked pained. "What have I done to you?"

"What do you mean?"

"You should be playing. See how these folks stopped everything to listen. And you never stopped grinning."

"Not just me...you too," Mike said, reaching across for her hands. "Besides, you're the one that makes me smile."

"Excuse me," the maître d' said, suddenly appearing at their table. "The hotel manager had to leave but said your meal is on the house and you could have a job playing anytime you like."

Mike chuckled. "Thanks for the offer but we're already employed."

The tuxedoed man nodded, smiled at Naomi and returned to his station.

Naomi silently studied Mike.

"What?" Mike said.

"Sure you don't need this?"

"I'm sure. Besides I have no idea what we're in for tomorrow." Mike paused and wiggled his eyebrows at her. "But before all that we need to get back to our love nest."

Naomi chuckled. "Must be the shortest honeymoon on record."

Mike smiled and reached to help her up. "We better get busy then."

𝄞

They could walk twenty minutes up the beach or drive the old Toyota pickup, left by her father, five minutes along a winding road to get to the orphanage school. With everything already set up, Naomi thought it fun to walk along the surf their first day.

"Nervous?" asked Naomi as they splashed barefoot, sand squishing between their toes.

"Scared to death," Mike said. "Don't think I've been this anxious since college wrestling matches."

Naomi guffawed. "You're four times their size. What are you worried about?"

"You're funny. What if they don't like me?"

"I'll be in the next room if you can't handle it."

Mike stopped suddenly and pulled her to him for a hug. "You are the bravest person I've ever known. Thank you for marrying me."

𝄞

Led by a harried nurse from the orphanage, eight kids showed up forty-five minutes late. Mike wasn't quite prepared for the rough condition of the children. When they came into the small courtyard in front of the schoolrooms they sat down on the dirt and looked aimlessly around.

Mike's heart sank.

The supervisor seemed eager to leave, so she quickly went over the list of names with Naomi and explained more kids might show up later in the week. The number of children would vary depending on their circumstances. Mike had the feeling the kids were deciding if they wanted to stay or not as they peered around – but Naomi didn't hesitate and moved into action.

"Good morning. I'm Naomi and this is my husband, Mike. We'll be your teachers for the next six months. But before we get into any schoolwork, I would like to know if anyone here is still hungry?"

A few hands went up.

Naomi had it all planned – food, fun, and music. She had bought a couple dozen cheap shorts and T-shirts and had records for the old hi-fi depending on the mood she wanted to set. And, of course, plenty of food for lunch and snacks.

"Would anybody like some sweet potato cookies and milk?"

This seemed to wake them up. Smiling, they all stood up from the ground.

"Good. But before I hand out the treats, I want everyone to pick out a pair of shorts and a T-shirt. Then we'll go around and meet everyone before we have a game of football (soccer). Those that don't want to play can draw or look at books on the tables at the back of the room. Then after lunch we'll do a little school work."

Genius, Mike thought. *Get their buy-in first. Then make learning fun and she'll have them hooked.*

By the end of the day, Mike was feeling more confident with most the kids laughing and gathering around him for attention. By the end of the first week all the kids but one showed up eager and ready to play and also learn a little something.

10
Reunion – Harlem, September

Planning a reunion was just what Rose needed. Persis and Jesse were living off on their own further up in the Sugar Hill neighborhood. Her youngest, Trina, was starting her freshman year at Cornell, Mike's alma mater. Always the matchmaker, Rose had Evette, one of the girls from church, help with the luncheon, thinking it would be good for a couple of the boys to see what a nice church girl looked like. And, who knows what could happen?

She could tell R.G. was in over his head with this gang so was hoping to get a handle on what was really going on and report to Mike that all was well. She was able to contact all the kids except Abby who was still in Europe with her parents. For a surprise, Rose got Liz Shepard to come. The leading actor in Mike's Broadway musical, she had helped prepare the kids for the Radio City competition. Liz said she would swing by and pick up R.G. on her way. With the dining room table spread with food and drinks, Rose went to answer the door, eager to hear all about how the rest of their summer had gone.

Jaz burst in cussing under her breath. Rose stood back flummoxed. She stepped out onto the stoop to meet Blake slogging up the stairs.

"Hello, Mrs. Monroe," he said stopping on a lower step looking up at her.

"Welcome, Blake." She turned to see where Jaz had headed. "What's with Jaz?"

"We had a little disagreement. She's not easy to get along with, you know."

Rose was searching for what to say when a cab pulled up with R.G. and Liz, all smiles.

Liz paid the cabby and shouted "hello" as she directed R.G. up the stairs. Rose gave him a warm hug and handed him off to Blake who was standing at the door.

"Any idea what's going on with Jaz?" Rose whispered into Liz's ear as they hugged.

"A lot. Some good but most not so good. R.G. filled me in."

"I'll catch up to you in a bit but, for now, would you please serve the drinks?"

Liz nodded and headed in.

Rose was about to close the door behind her when Tobias and Carlos called out, running up the sidewalk. Rose was happy to see their smiling faces.

She stepped back out to gigantic hugs from the two boys.

"So good to see you, Mrs. M," they said in unison.

Rose held the face of each one and kissed them on the forehead. "Is it possible you two have gotten better looking in the last two months?"

"I don't know about the wet-back, but it's possible I –"

"Tobias!" Rose scolded. "That's demeaning. What has gotten into you?"

Tobias puckered his lips and looked at his shoes. "Just joking, ma'am."

Rose narrowed her eyes. "Think about it. Would you say that in front of his parents?"

He shook his head.

"You're good boys. Remember words have power, to lift or bring down," Rose said, then gave them a redemptive smile. "Looking forward to hearing what you've been working on."

They nodded thoughtfully and Rose followed them into the house.

Rose was glad to see everyone remembered to bring their instruments but wasn't sure what to do for drums when Cobi showed up with his drum sticks poking out his back pocket.

Evette had snacks set up and directed the boys to the dining room on the right. Rose smiled as she caught an approving look from both Carlos and Tobias.

Across the hall from the dining room, Blake had apparently found comfort sitting alone at the living room piano. Jaz was lounging on the couch looking around at nothing in particular. Rose moved into action and headed for Jaz while Liz went to sit with Blake.

"How have you been, dear?" Rose asked, sitting down next to her.

Jaz manufactured a slight smile. "Not bad. Playing at Johnny's with Blake," she said, her eyes skyward with a slight nod across the room in Blake's direction.

"How's your mother doing?"

"Okay I guess. Don't see her much now that Blake and I have a place."

Rose let that news hang for a beat. "Oh. Thought he was headed for college. And what happened with him and Abby?"

"His parents kicked his butt out because he wanted to pursue music instead of medicine. And Abby, who knows. Guess she'd rather be with her parents in Europe."

Rose couldn't help but make a face.

"He made the right choice. He loves music," Jaz added, defensively.

Rose couldn't help herself. "You two an item now?"

"You mean are we doing it? Hardly – not that Blake wouldn't consider it though."

Before Rose could respond a loud thumping came from the front door. When Rose answered, Travis and Mia stood silently with their instruments – Cobi behind them was pulsing to a beat somewhere inside him.

After hugs all around, Rose immediately picked up on Mia's angst. Travis as usual was quiet and unreadable.

Rose got everyone's attention, after closing the door. "I can't wait to hear all about what's been going on with you all. So why don't we head to the table and you can tell me all about it while we eat."

The kids sauntered to the dining room, spiritless. Rose looked to Liz for a clue. Liz hunched and shook her head.

𝄞

When the last of the kids had left Rose joined Liz and R.G. in the living room.

"Well…that was a bust. I thought it would be fun for them to reconnect," Rose said, dropping into a living room chair.

"Don't know what's happen to um," R.G said. "Maybe they got spoilt, winning the competition."

"Let me see if I have this straight," Rose said, looking back and forth from Liz to R.G. "Mia is depressed because she didn't get into Julliard. Travis, sullen, acting like he's stuck somehow. Tobias, Carlos and Cobi have given up on their band idea because their mentor, Garrett, left on tour. That leaves the love triangle between Blake, Jaz and Abby. I am not sure where that boy's head is. What's he going to do when Abby returns?" Rose closed her eyes and moaned. "What's happened to these kids? They're all stumbling around aimless." She looked over at Liz and R.G. "What am I going to tell Mike?"

11

Tempest – Monrovia, September

After a couple weeks at the school, Mike was finally able to relax – confirming that children love making music no matter their background. One thing did gnaw at him though; his mother hadn't been completely forthcoming about the Y kids when they talked on the phone. 'Everyone was doing fine.' He wasn't so sure.

"What's the long face about?" asked Naomi, coming up to him as he sat on the porch with his Sunday morning coffee.

He pulled back from staring out to sea. "Something's not right with the kids."

"Of course. They've been neglected all their lives, but I'm thinking they're much happier now."

Mike shook his head. "No. I'm thinking about the Y kids. Mother talked all about what they were doing without any joy in her voice. She's hiding something."

Naomi was silent for a moment. "Sorry. I know you miss them. Maybe we should fly back for Christmas." She peered down at him. "Would that be okay?"

A little smile rose on Mike's face. "Yes. That would be good."

Naomi moved in front of him and squirmed her way onto his lap, squeezed his cheeks and kissed him. "I've got another good idea if you want to hear it."

Mike's slight smile turned into a broad grin. He raised his eyebrows and nodded in the direction of the bedroom.

She nodded back with a grin of her own.

𝄞

After they had walked to the school Monday morning, a dark bank of tumbling clouds with wispy claw-like fingers suddenly appeared, hanging low over the ocean.

Mike peered at the sky as they stood on the beach in front of the school. "That doesn't look good."

"Well, you said you like storms," Naomi said, turning to the classroom as a gust of wind snapped a branch off a nearby tree. "Hope the kids get here soon."

Feeling vulnerable, Mike hustled into his classroom. The simply built structure was nothing more than a two-by-four construction with corrugated sheets of metal for a roof and siding, all resting on a six-inch concrete slab. Mike ran into Naomi's adjoining room. "You get hurricanes here?"

She gave Mike a grim look. "Not hurricanes. But –."

Just then the door burst open with a herd of shouting children. Fright torn across the supervisor's face.

"Mr. Monroe, just as we pulled up the radio announced a severe tropical storm warning." She ran to the window and looked out at the beach and the fast moving front.

Naomi gathered all the kids into her room and did a quick head count. "I count eleven. Is that right, Miss Abina?"

"Yes. Noah disappeared again over the weekend."

Mike started to pace in front of the window. "From the looks of it we have just minutes to find someplace to hunker down."

"Should I head back with them?" Abina asked.

"No," Naomi responded. "Too dangerous in that flimsy bus."

Mike rushed out the classroom door to try and find something studier than the rickety glorified shed they were in. Mike scanned the courtyard. It was obvious their best bet would be the low cement block structure that housed the pump house and bathrooms.

He ran back in to tell Naomi. Just as she turned to him a powerful blast hit causing the building to shudder and lean away from the wind. The roof began to rattle like a thousand flaying chains as a large branch tore away from a fifty-foot baobab tree and smashed through the west-facing window. Shards of glass shot into the room like a machine gun blast – pelting Mike's back as he turned to shield a child.

"To the bathrooms!" he shouted, scooping up two small kids, one under each arm. They made it out of the classroom and across the courtyard with Naomi following – shepherding as best she could the last of the children. Mike fought the bathroom door to keep it open until the last child was inside.

"What happened to Abina?" Mike yelled above the roar of the wind.

He cracked the door open to look for her. The wind and rain pushed back with a hellish vengeance.

"Don't go out there, Mike!" Naomi screamed.

Mike hesitated a moment then squeezed through the narrow opening – wincing from the daggers of glass in his back that pushed deeper into his flesh.

Through the assaulting deluge he saw Abina coming across the courtyard from the bus. She was barely able to make headway as she leaned into the growling torrent, rain soaked leaves plastered against her.

Suddenly Mike felt the ground shake like a grenade had gone off. The giant baobab tree had split in two with a crack and slammed down on the metal roof of the school. Sheets of corrugated roof panels were flung into the air – deadly spinning blades of steel.

Mike saw it as if in slow motion. He pushed off from the cement block pump-house driving his legs like pistons to reach Abina. She turned to his shout as he leaped the last six feet to pull her to the ground. A serrated blade of a roof panel hurled through the air slicing just inches over their heads. As Mike covered her, more loose chunks of wood and glass flew past. He looked over her shoulder to see what was left of the school – the one remaining wall could easily topple and launch more debris. They had to move. NOW!

Mike grabbed Abina's shirt, practically ripping it off, and yanked her stumbling to her feet and over to the pump-house. Naomi had been peering through a crack in the door taking in the scene. She fought to keep it open as they staggered in, landing on the floor in a heap.

Naomi gasped. Mike's shoulder and back were bloodied from glistening wedges of window glass sticking out of his shirt.

"How long is this going to last?" Mike shouted. "Looks like we need to get to the doc with a couple of the kids."

"And you," Naomi said.

Mike looked hard at Abina trying to control his anger. "What were you thinking? You should have headed for shelter with us."

"Sorry, Mr. Monroe," Abina said, tears in her eyes. "Had to get Folami's medicine. I was afraid his asthma would flare up, stressing about the storm. Can't stand to see him choke."

Mike closed his eyes and took a breath. "Sorry for yelling at you. I didn't know."

Abina dropped her eyes and nodded.

"Mike! Blood is dripping off your arm."

"My back's killing me," he said, his shirt soaked with a growing patch of blood.

"Oh Lord…we got to stop the blood pouring out of you."

"Probably a good idea. I'm feeling faint." Mike swayed and leaned over on his side.

Naomi started to tremble – her mouth open, gasping.

"I've got this Naomi. I'm also the nurse at the orphanage," Abina said, going for the first aid kit in the bathroom storage closet.

$\oint$

As the storm raged, Mike and Naomi and Abina huddled with the kids and prayed. Snuggled together in the confined darkness the children fell asleep, arms and legs entwined like a litter of puppies.

12
La Familia -Manhattan, September

An unexpected knock at the door pulled Blake away from the small electric keyboard he was renting for twenty-five dollars a week. They never had a visitor so he couldn't imagine who it could be.

"Hello, Blake."

Blake stood wide-eyed with the doorknob still in his hand, trying to get his mouth to work.

"Abby?"

She stood a moment with her eyebrows arched. "You going to let me in?"

He took a quick glance over his shoulder. "Sure. Why not."

Abby tilted her head and peered past him then slid through the half opened door and stopped to take in the sparse furnishings – a huge beat up couch straight ahead under the window, a daybed in the left hand corner and a kitchenette and small wood table and chairs on the right.

"Sorry. I didn't know you were coming back so soon." Blake racked his brain for what to do next.

"I know. I talked my parents into letting me return as long as I promise to get serious about auditions at Julliard or MSM. Besides, there's nothing for me in Europe."

Blake was beginning to sweat. "Ah, you know…why don't we run down to Reggio's for a coffee. They've got amazing cappuccino. You ever have one?"

Abby squinted at him. "Yeah. I just spent two months in Italy. They invented it you know."

"Oh…of course. Let me get my wallet and we'll go."

Blake took three steps toward the bedroom when Jaz burst out wrapped in a bath towel with her hairbrush in her hand.

"Dammit, Blake…you using my hairbrush again?" she asked, shaking the brush at him. Stopping mid-shake, she tipped her head in Abby's direction. "Well…well," offering her smirkiest of smirks. "You didn't mention we were having company."

$$\oint$$

The slam of the back door caused Carlos' eyes to widen.

"Crap…dad's home early."

"So?" Tobias said, hunching his shoulders.

"I'm supposed to be at JC studying economics."

"Economics? Why…?" Tobias shook his head in disbelief.

Carlos hung his head. "I don't know. I had to sign up for something."

"Brilliant man. You think studying about money will get you some?"

Carlos put his finger to his lips and whispered. "Shut up."

The clomping of work boots crossed the kitchen floor above them. Tobias put his hand to his mouth like he was about to break out laughing.

Carlos raised his fist, threatening to slug the bass player. The boots started downstairs then stopped when the phone rang. The boots went back up and into the hall to the phone.

Carlos motioned to Tobias to put down his bass and follow him up a couple steps to the side door leading to the driveway.

Tobias was about to lose it. Carlos threatened with gritted teeth and his hands gripped like he was about to strangle him.

Stepping lightly they made it up the stairs and out the door, closing it gently. Turning to the right they jogged down the driveway to the garage and around to the alley. Out of sight, Carlos fell against the back wall and slid to the ground, cradling his head in his hands. Tobias looked down at him and rolled his eyes.

"You're pathetic you know. Get some balls and tell your folks what you want to do with your life."

Carlos looked up. "Easy for you to say. You're not the first in your whole family to go to college." Carlos couldn't help but snort. "Okay, junior college. That counts doesn't it?"

"Sure it does man. You're awesome," Tobias said, dropping down next to him, covering his mouth, laughing into his hand.

"You're an idiot," Carlos said and punched his best friend in the arm – hard.

𝄞

Once again Cobi vowed not to go drinking with his pals after work. Working for his uncle hanging drywall all day with a hangover wasn't his idea of fun. But after a shower and a massive plate of leftover linguini with marinara sauce he was ready for another night with his old high school buddies who could always find someone to buy beer for the evening. The spirited nights made the drudgery of the days tolerable. But he did need to check in with *La Familia* from the YMCA to see if anyone was getting work performing. *Who am I kidding? Who would hire any of us?*

$$\textit{\&}$$

Mia didn't want to get her hopes up. Travis said he had something interesting to talk about. But why wouldn't he just tell her on the phone?

She hadn't been to the Y since the last practice of *La Familia* before playing at Radio City. Walking in the entrance she saw Travis sitting by the window in the small café to the left, wearing a black turtleneck and flared Levi's with his afro exploding in a halo about his smooth handsome face. He stood with a broad grin and pulled out a chair for her. It was so good to see him she wanted to hug him but he shied, not moving too close. She gave him an affectionate smile instead.

"Hi, Travis," she said, putting her hand on his as he held the chair.

"Man…its good to see you," his eyes sparkling with hope.

Mia sat down dropping her shoulder bag on the chair next to her. "You look great. Tell me what you've been doing since Radio City."

"That's what I want to talk to you about. There's a position that opened up at the Winter Garden Theater where I'm playing. The cellist broke her leg in an accident and the backup already has taken a job overseas. So they are desperate for a replacement."

Mia's eyes grew wide and stared at him, mouth open. "Are you saying I should try out?"

"Of course. You're amazing."

Mia squinted at him. "Why would they hire me? I don't have a degree. I've never played other than in high school and *La Familia*."

"Relax." Travis said, holding up his hands. "First, I know you can do this. Second, Michael Monroe, one of New York's renowned musicians, has mentored you. And…you played a big part in winning first at the Radio City competition. But, best of all, it's an open audition so they'll judge you on what you can do not on what you've done."

Mia's heart quickened with Travis' proposal. Not so much from the possibility of playing at the theater but from gazing into his smiling caramel eyes.

13

Noah – Monrovia, September

Mike grunted as he nudged open the door of their concrete block shelter. Twisted limbs and scraps of lumber where stacked against it from the storm. He was finally able to squeeze through and pull away some debris to get the kids out. The sky was now a brilliant blue backdrop against a scene of mud, branches, splintered lumber and scattered panels of roof and siding. The only thing left standing on the concrete slab, besides a scatter of overturned chairs and desks, was the old upright piano – leaves plastered against the soundboard, the bench nowhere in sight. Mike caught Naomi's eye as she came out the door. He went over to hold her. She pulled her hands to her face – eyes wide in disbelief.

"Everyone is safe," he whispered.

She took in a long breath with the kids crowding around them like a brood of chicks then narrowed her eyes with the look of a warrior.

"We need to get the kids back to the orphanage to see if they would be safe there. They could get hurt around here with all the broken glass and splinters of wood."

Miraculously the old beater bus only had a few small branches lying on the hood and choked to life after the third try.

$\oint$

Sheltered from a dense stand of hundred foot azobe trees, the orphanage had suffered very little damage. After getting the kids back safely, Mike and Naomi had Abina drop them back at what was left of the school. They put off discussing what all this meant for them, instead went to work on saving anything of value, which wasn't much. As they stood in the remains of the classroom eating sandwiches from the orphanage, they heard a rustle in the bushes behind them. Naomi reached over and grabbed Mike's hand and squeezed – harder as the sound got louder. There appeared first a small forearm then a shoulder attached to a skinny black boy with a bloody shirt wrapped from under his chin over his head as if he had a toothache. His eyes grew wide like a feral animal when he saw them looking at him. He froze for a moment then ducked back into the bushes. Naomi glanced at Mike then ran after the child.

"Boy. Don't go!" she shouted in Liberian Pidgin English jumping off the concrete slab of the school. Crashing into the thick foliage she stumbled over a mangrove root and went sprawling face first into a shallow swampy puddle. She lifted her head up – gasping and cussing in local dialect. Mike followed after her jumping over the offending exposed root to find her spread-eagled, spitting out muddy swamp water. Looking like he was about to burst out laughing he reached down to help her up. But instead of getting to her feet she gave Mike a good yank pulling him into the muck next to her.

"Crap!" Mike hollered coming up for air. "You... you, you."

Naomi sat up and gave him a snarl. "You were going to laugh at me weren't you?"

Mike sat up next to her and slapped the water with his hands. "No!"

She kept her snarl.

Mike tucked his chin down. "Sorry." Then he glanced at her. "Boy…do you know how to cuss. Think that's what I heard."

"Shut up and help me up."

Mud and leaves dripped from them as they made their way back to what was left of the school, picking up a couple chairs that had blown off the slab.

Setting the chairs at the piano, Mike turned and faced Naomi. "Who do you suppose that was?"

Naomi winced and shook her head. "Haven't seen him before but it looked like he might be hurt. He sure can run though." She looked in the direction where the child disappeared.

Mike couldn't resist plunking a couple keys to check out the foliage-adorned piano. It sounded just fine. He adjusted his chair to reach the pedals and played *You Are My Sunshine* – leaning back with his eyes closed. He had leaves and mud clumps clinging to his hair giving him a look of some sort of mythological forest creature, but a benevolent one. The sight of him playing like he was on stage at Lincoln Center as if nothing had happened caused Naomi's heart to swell. She pulled her chair up next to him and embellished the simple melody with wispy arpeggios in the upper register – a slight smile appearing along with a deep sigh. They carried on for another ten minutes, the mud drying on them from the warm sunlight beaming like a spotlight through what was left of the baobab tree.

When Mike lifted his hands from the last chord of *Georgia On My Mind*, he reached around her and pulled her in for a long kiss. As Naomi sighed from his tenderness, a stifled snicker came from the bushes they had plunged through earlier.

Naomi froze. Only moving her eyes she caught a glimpse of a blood stained shirt and the smiling soft face of the mystery boy peering out from the bushes.

"Hello, there," she called out sweetly. "What's your name?"

The face disappeared.

"Come on now." Naomi stood up. "I'm not going to chase you. See what happened last time." She motioned at her clothes and waited.

The little face peered out again, ten yards to the right.

"What's your name child?"

"Noah!" came a shout. Naomi snorted and looked at Mike.

"Well, Noah, you don't sound shy to me. Why don't you come here?"

"No!"

Mike held up a hand to Naomi and stood from the chair. "Noah, would you like to come to dinner with us? We'll have your favorite thing to eat if you tell us what that is."

The face disappeared again for a moment along with some rustling. Then a skinny boy of about six or seven stepped out a couple feet with a small bag of something; stopped and looked hard at them. All three stared silently for what seemed minutes. Naomi tilted her head and smiled. Mike put his arm around her.

It seemed the boy tried to resist while being drawn to them by some invisible force. He moved slowly through the mud and around downed limbs and stood in front of them, silent as a statue.

The face of this beautiful brown-eyed boy gave no hints of what lay inside. No guile. No joy. Just an emptiness that seemed bottomless. His smooth ebony skin stretched over his limbs and cheekbones. It seemed you could wave your hand through him as if he was an apparition.

"What's in the bag, Noah?" Naomi asked, her hand reaching for her heart.

"Stuff."

Naomi smiled up at Mike then to Noah. "You know, Noah, if you want we could go to our house and get you something to eat. Does that sound good?"

Noah glanced toward the bushes then at Naomi and hunched his shoulders.

"Okay," she said. "We live not far down the beach. So just follow us."

Noah looked around like he was considering a better offer. Naomi reached for Mike's hand and they started walking through the debris to the beach. After a moment of deliberation Noah decided to follow – about twenty paces behind.

14

Dirt – Manhattan, September

"**S**o…you say my talent is God-given. Don't I have anything to do with it?" Jaz said, sitting down at the piano bench with her head cocked back. She had stopped by R.G.'s to pick up some saxophone reeds on the way to the YMCA to meet up with *La Familia*.

"Of course. It's your job to use it. Otherwise it serves no purpose."

"I don't know…."

R.G. humphed. "Get me that plant by the window and bring it here."

"Oookay…" she said, and got up to pick it up off the shelf. "Amazing it's still alive."

Jaz brought the small pot back and placed it in R.G.'s open hand as he sat at the kitchen table.

"I keep it watered, Jaz. When you can't see, your nose can guide you and memory… your sight."

R.G. held the plant to his nose and smelled it. "See what a hand full of dirt can do. It's miracle stuff. Dirt can grow a stalk of wheat for bread…or a giant redwood to build a house.

If God can put that into motion, He *surely* can pass out gifts to his people."

Jaz paused a moment. "I do like the dirt analogy. Most days that's exactly how I feel...like so much dirt."

"Listen to me," R.G. snapped, but then took in a long slow breath. "How you gonna use your gift? Feed folks with it or grow weeds? Music can heal, Jaz."

R.G. dropped his head. "I know you know that." He held out his hand hoping she would take it and she did. "It's not just about you. When you play you touch my soul and others as well. It carries us away in light if only for a little while."

R.G. lightly squeezed her hand. "I know you miss your father. He was a good man before crack. 'Tis hard...not to die with those we've lost."

Jaz remained silent.

Abby and Blake sat at the Y café to meet up with *La Familia* for a practice session. Blake had called everyone to see if they would be interested in getting work playing at weddings. That and he hoped to find out where he stood with Abby.

Silent, Abby sat across from Blake gazing out the window. She had left his apartment without a word after seeing Jaz come out of the bathroom in only a towel. Thankful she even showed up, Blake was hoping to set things straight…but sensed something had changed between them.

"You have to understand. I had no idea how long you'd be gone and after a blowout with my parents I needed a place to live so I moved in with R.G. and Jaz." He tipped his head and studied Abby to see if there was any hint of understanding. Nothing. "But it was really too tight for three people so after a couple weeks we pooled our money to get our own place." Blake paused and nibbled his lip. "Abby, trust me there's nothing going on. You know Jaz. She's a loner."

Abby finally shifted her eyes from the window and locked in on him. "It was just a shock. I thought she and I had finally made peace after playing at the competition. But seeing her that day ...I don't know. She gave me that snarky look of hers."

He reached across to hold her hand and changed the subject. "Tell me about Europe. How are your parents? Do you have to go back soon?"

Abby pulled her hand back and picked up her cup. She sipped her tea for a moment then set it down. The Abby he knew gradually appeared as she began telling him all about her time taking lessons and traveling. How her parents were thinking of buying an apartment in Florence because they spend so much time there, but she had convinced them to let her move back with Nana, her grandmother, on Long Island and audition for either MSM or Julliard in the spring. In the meantime she would keep practicing her violin as well as take voice lessons after finding how much she loved singing at Persis' wedding. Blake saw an opening to tell her his idea of getting work for the band doing weddings. And filled her in on his breakup with his parents.

Blake paused and sat back to get her vibe. "So...are we okay?"

Abby looked away. They sat in silence for a moment until Cobi, Travis and Mia rushed up practically crashing into them.

"Man, it's good to see you," Cobi shouted, looking only at Abby. "Hope you're here to stay."

"Yeah, I'm not going anywhere," Blake said, before Abby could answer.

"Oh...hey, Blake," Cobi said while he grabbed a chair from the next table and leaned over the back of it grinning at Abby. Abby simpered.

Travis pulled over another table and a couple chairs. Mia sat down looking like she was sorting out what was going on between Cobi, Abby and Blake.

"How are you guys?" Blake asked Mia and Travis, to get the attention away from Cobi. "Hear you got a *real* job playing at the Winter Garden Theater."

"Hey, Johnny's is real work. Just a little smokier," Travis said. "But, where's Jaz? I heard you two were an item."

Blake sputtered and flashed a glance at Abby. "She'll be here any minute but let's get something straight. We're just sharing an apartment, nothing else."

Travis snorted at Blake's defensive tone. "Oookay...I see," and turned his face to hide a smirk.

There was a moment of silence between them until pounding jerked everyone's attention to the large plate-glass window looking onto 23rd. Jumping up and down like a circus clown was Tobias with Carlos pressing his lips to the window and puffing out his cheeks like a blowfish; causing shrieks of joy as they got up and ran to greet the two guitarists at the front door.

After high-fives and hugs all around they got the key from the information desk and headed up to the *practice closet*, as they called it, that Mike had negotiated with the YMCA for his young musicians. The storage room – wall-to-wall shelving on both sides packed with boxes of supplies and reference books – was just big enough for the eight of them with a basic four piece drum set in the back corner and a battered but in tune studio upright piano just inside the door on the left.

They all stopped and peered around the cramped storage room in quiet reverence for all the hours they had spent rehearsing for the Radio City competition – that turned out to be the most memorable time in their young lives.

Blake, hoping to get things started on a positive note, went to the piano and pounded out a brief intro to get everyone's attention.

"Okay, guess we should decide what we want to work on. Anyone bring music to try out?"

Just then Jaz burst in and stood at the door appearing dressed for a gang war: black headband and hooded black sweatshirt under a black leather jacket scrawled with graffiti, scuffed combat boots and tattered Levi's – holding her sax case with a bloody hand.

"Sorry for being late. Some bastard tried to steal my sax when I cut through the ally," she said as if it was no big deal.

Blake winced. "Your hand...you all right? It's dripping blood."

"Just a scrape. I'll wrap it with something," she said.

Everyone looked on as she dropped her case on the desk by the door, wrapped her hand with her headband and took off her jacket and sweatshirt. Jaz turned around with her sax and caught everyone staring at her.

"What the hell? We gonna play something or what?"

Everyone turned at once like woken from a stupor and went about setting up. Blake faced them at the piano on the left. Arcing in front of him were Abby (violin), Mia (cello) and Jaz (sax) in the first row; Tobias (guitar), Carlos (bass guitar) and Travis (trumpet) behind the three girls; then Cobi (drums) in the back right corner. Blake couldn't help but smile seeing the group together again.

When the cacophony of tune up and the kibitzing died down, Blake leaned over the old upright. "I brought the music we played at Persis' wedding as a warm up unless somebody has a better idea."

"Wait a minute, Blake." Jaz stood up and let her sax hang in front of her. "You know... before we go to all the trouble of practicing, shouldn't we see if everyone is committed to taking *La Familia* on the road. Otherwise we're just wasting time here."

"Jaz," Cobi said standing from behind his drums. "What's wrong with just having some fun? So what if we might not get work."

"I don't know about you, man, but I'm in this to make some coin."

Cobi groaned, flipped a drumstick up and caught it. "Still a pain in the butt. Why would I expect anything different?"

"Just sayin'. I don't have time to do this half-assed."

Abby moaned and shook her head. Jaz stepped in front of her and glared down. "I understand you don't need to be concerned about making a living, but I do."

Abby stood up facing Jaz – staring.

"What?" Jaz sneered.

"Do you have to go through your poor struggling musician routine…again?"

"Sit down, Abby," Jaz said and nudged her with her shoulder. Catching her off balance, Abby fell back on the edge of her chair that scooted out from under her. Trying not to drop her violin she rolled over onto floor with her hand outstretched, holding up her instrument.

"What's *wrong* with you!" Cobi hollered, charging out from behind the drums to get to Abby, colliding with Jaz sending her headlong into the back of the piano with a crack. Blake leaped from around the piano and grabbed Cobi by the shirt and started yelling and shaking him. Jaz sprung up with a gash in her head and was about attack Cobi when six-foot-three Travis grabbed five-foot-two Jaz from behind – her feet flailing in rage. Mia, cradling her cello, headed for the door, grabbing her case on the way out.

Everyone was now screaming with Tobias and Carlos jumping in to tear Cobi and Blake apart as chairs and music stands went flying.

"You're a maniac!" Abby screamed, staggering around to find her violin case amongst the chaos.

Suddenly a thunderous blast came from the door like the hinges had been blown off. "What the hell's goin' on here!" boomed an immense security guard, a billy club in hand.

16
Passage – Monrovia, September

Noah had only occasionally shown up at the orphanage, but usually disappeared after the evening meal. The staff finally gave up trying to convince him to stay. He seemed to be in another world, rarely making eye contact – his intelligent dark eyes assessing those around him with the scrutiny of someone many years older.

Noah had been observing the goings on at the school, undetected amongst the trees, drawn to the music that wafted out the windows of Mike's classroom. He enjoyed watching the world from a distance not having to take part – safe. He would not allow himself to be taken advantage of again.

He wasn't sure why he trusted these people. Yes he was hungry, but they were somehow different. He was puzzled but curious. He liked the way they treated each other, holding hands as they walked away. It seemed he didn't have a choice but to follow them.

𝄞

Despite its dilapidated appearance the sturdy little beach bungalow, nestled in the edge of the rainforest, had survived the storm remarkably well – just a toppled palm tree out front and a few shingles pealed off the roof. After Mike cleaned out branches and palm fronds from their open-air porch, Naomi served a Liberian dinner she thought Noah would like: rice, sweet potato, spicy stew, and fried plantains.

"Well, what did you think of my wife's cook'n?" Mike asked, pointing to Noah's empty plate as they sat at the porch table – a four foot purplish slab of Azobe wood, salvaged from a construction site and mounted on an old oak barrel.

Noah puckered his mouth and hunched his shoulders.

"Okay…I'll assume it met your approval," Mike offered.

A little nod and a slight grin from Noah was all Mike got.

Despite his age there was something about this child that reminded Mike of Jaz; self-reliant yet sensitive. Naomi held her face as she sat across the table watching the one-sided conversation, a slight grin tickling the edge of her mouth.

Mike coaxed Noah to sit with him on the couch to look at picture books while Naomi made up a bed in the guest room with a nightlight on the side table.

Naomi came out of the bedroom and sat on the other side of Noah.

"Got a bed waiting for you if you like. And maybe tomorrow after breakfast we could go into town and do some shopping."

Noah twisted to look up at each of them then sunk back into the couch and looked down at his bare feet.

Naomi peered at his callouses and moaned. "Maybe we could find some shoes you like then go to the market and buy something for dinner."

Noah gazed off like he was envisioning a dream

"So, what do you think? Want to spend the night and help us shop tomorrow?"

Noah tucked his chin in, started to grin and nodded.

Mike looked over at Naomi. "Is that a yes, then?"

Noah peeked up at Mike with smiling eyes and said, "yes."

Mike lept up and clapped his hands in front of Noah and whooped, "I told you this boy could talk! Isn't he wonderful?" Mike laughed and reached for Noah's hand. "Come on…let's go for a run on the beach before bedtime. Maybe Naomi would have some milk and sweet potato cookies when we get back."

Naomi smiled and nodded. "I could do that."

There was hardly a need for discussion after putting Noah to bed that evening. They could see it in each other's eyes. This child deserved a home.

Naomi called Abina to report that Noah was with them. While on the phone, Abina told her that clearly Noah met orphan status and was adoptable. He had been abandoned and living on the streets for two years with no living relatives.

𝄞

Mike woke the next morning feeling eyes on him. He rolled over to see Noah standing next to the bed staring expressionless at him. Mike couldn't help but snort as he nudged Naomi in the back to wake her. Naomi moaned and looked over her shoulder at Mike. Seeing Noah her eyes widened. She scooted over to make room and gestured for Noah to jump in between them. He shook his head.

"Oh, come on," Mike said, patting the bed with his hand.

Noah still wasn't sure so moved to the foot of the bed and crawled up near their feet.

"Well, that's a start," Mike said. Then after a glance at Naomi he sat up and leaned back on the headboard and caught Noah's gaze.

"How would you like to come live with us, Noah?"

Noah again gave them his "okay, I guess", shoulder shrug.

Mike grinned, broadly. "Alright then, but you have to give me at least two words in a row first."

Noah looked deep into Mike eyes and asked softly, "How long?"

As soon as Mike opened the door for Abina the next morning she reached out and hugged him with a squeeze that took his breath away then leaned back with a great sigh.

"I've feared for that boy ever since he showed up at the orphanage. He's such a loner and wouldn't let anyone close to him. Seems you've been chosen, like he's been waiting for you all along."

With Noah outside climbing a tree, Abina sat with Mike and Naomi going over all the paperwork for adoption. Because they already had government background checks as teachers and with Abina's recommendation they met the requirements of the Liberian Ministry of Justice as adoptive parents. Mike could have his mother expedite the process in the U.S. by contacting Alliance for Children, an adoption service provider in New York to handle the paperwork on that end. All in all it looked like it would take no more than three or four weeks before the adoption was finalized. In the meantime Noah could stay with them. Abina already had his birth certificate but needed to get a Liberian passport, exit clearance, medical exam and a U.S. Immigration visa through the embassy.

Before Abina left for the orphanage, they went outside looking for Noah so he could say goodbye to her. Naomi stood on the porch and gave out a motherly call. "Nooooah."

Nothing.

"Noah! Come here, Miss Abina is leaving," she said with more urgency.

Mike glanced at Naomi and sprang off the porch and out into the woods followed by the two women calling Noah's name.

After twenty minutes of the three running frantically through the woods and up and down the beach they met back at the house – only to find Noah sitting in the porch chair swinging his legs with a big grin. So began their initiation into parenthood.

Naomi, first relieved then angry, ran onto the porch and stopped in front of her renegade soon-to-be-son not knowing if she should hug or spank the child. She decided to do neither but stood looking down letting him see how his little prank had hurt her – her face pained with tears. Mike and Abina stood in their places, watching. Noah's grin slowly turned into quivering lips as he squeezed his eyes shut. Mike walked up to Naomi and put his arm around her and said, "We love you, Noah. Please don't do that again."

Naomi knelt down in front of him and turned his face to her as she smiled. Noah burst out of the chair into her arms. Mike reached out to Abina who looked like she needed a hug as tears dripped off her chin.

𝄞

After Abina left, Naomi put together a list of things to buy for Noah: shoes, socks, underwear, pants, shirts, toothbrush and other necessities – a bookstore to see what might interest him and a market to let him choose food for dinner.

As they were walking out to the old Toyota pickup, a black and white police car crunched up the gravel driveway and parked behind them blocking their path. An officer got out and solemnly walked up to them and addressed Naomi.

"Are you Naomi Roberts?"

Naomi glanced over at Mike then at the officer. "That's me."

17

Harlem - October

Tears of joy from the small reception party could have filled a bucket as Naomi and Mike, with Noah asleep in Mike's arms, came out the jet-way at Kennedy Airport. Rose couldn't wait another second and pushed her way through exiting passengers to get to her grandson, with Mike's sisters and Jesse trailing close behind her. Friends from church chose to stay out of the way holding balloons and a 'Welcome to America, Noah' banner.

The visit by the Monrovia Police officer only confirmed what Naomi knew in her gut; her father had been found murdered. There was no trace of the money. And with no money the orphan school would be put on hold. This left Naomi and Mike with no reason to stay longer than to have a funeral for her father and complete the adoption process. But they now understood the real purpose for them going to Liberia. And that was in Mike's arms.

"Oh…my sweet baby," Rose said, stopping in front of them stroking Noah's back as she gave Mike and Naomi a peck on the cheek.

"Mother. He's not a baby. He's almost seven. Just small for his age."

"Give him to me."

"Go sit down and I will. He's not as light as he looks."

His mother beamed when Mike lowered the sleeping child into her arms then he and Naomi circulated around the gathering that had come to witness their homecoming.

Noah woke minutes later with a gasp seeing a strange person holding him. His head swiveled around and he immediately reached out to Naomi sitting next to him. Crawling into her arms, his eyes grew wide as he studied all the smiling people staring at him. Then he let out a sigh…seeing his father come up to him.

It only took the ride from the airport to their home in Harlem for Rose to win Noah over. By the time they arrived at the Strivers Row townhouse, Mike driving the family station wagon, Noah had crept back into her lap and fallen asleep as she hummed hymns and rocked him.

Mike pulled up front of the classic brownstone hoping his son would approve.

"Here we are, Noah. This is your new home," Mike said, getting out and opening the back door.

Still in his grandma's lap, Noah peered up at Mike then squinted out at the three-story row house – the autumn yellow-orange leaves of the honey locust trees casting golden afternoon light. Noah reached for Mike's hand and stepped out. Naomi slid out from the front seat and grabbed Noah's other hand and they walked to the stairs. Getting to the first step they swung their thin forty-five pound son up to the second step causing him to giggle. He then broke loose and scrambled on all fours up the remaining steps and stood on the top stoop looking out, cranking his head back and forth – surveying the street. He looked down at Mike, Naomi and Rose with a smile that warmed their hearts then ran back down to them for a hug. It was apparent Noah approved of his new home and he hadn't even gotten in the door yet.

$\natural$

Even though Mike didn't sleep well on the eleven-hour nonstop flight to New York, he could hardly wait to check on the Y-kids but first wanted to get Noah set up in his old bedroom. It still had posters of his favorite musicians on the wall and wrestling trophies on the dresser. After a tour of the downstairs living room, dining room and kitchen, Mike led Noah upstairs to his bedroom, first door on the right on the landing overlooking the living room.

Trina, being the artistic one in the family, had drawn a fancy graphic for the door: Noah's Room. Mike stopped at the door pointing to the sign.

"This is your room now. It was mine when I was growing up but now it's all yours," he said and opened the door to sunlight streaming in from the small backyard.

Rose had dug out the old toy box from the basement and had it sitting out with the lid open against the left wall. The box was filled with Mike's old toys: wooden blocks, Tonka trucks, Legos, action figures and Matchbox cars. Straight ahead was Mike's desk and chair in front of the window, the shelves on both sides full of picture books and games. In the corner to the right was the dresser and bed with a colorful bedspread and rug that Rose and Persis had fun picking out.

Noah stood at the door appraising the situation.

"Go in and try out the bed to see if it fits," Mike said.

Noah caught the joke and went in to stretch out in the middle and reached out with his arms and legs for the sides of the bed and nodded an "okay".

Mike laughed and went to sit on the edge of the bed.

"You know…you're going to have to start using more words. Not everyone is a mind reader like me."

Noah chuckled. "I like the bed. It fits good."

"Good." Mike couldn't wait to show off his son to the Y-kids so asked Noah if he would like to go with him downtown to meet up with some friends.

Noah sat up and started to shrug his shoulders then stopped. Holding back a giggle, he said, "Yes, sir. That's good."

Mike threw back his head with a snort. "Okay, Noah, no more calling me sir. That makes me feel like an old man. Would it be okay if you called me…I don't know…how about Daddy, Dad, Father, Papa or Pop? I called my father, Dad."

Noah looked out the window then back at Mike. "Papa?"

"Papa sounds good to me and you have already chosen Mama for your mother. And I *know* she loves you calling her that. Now you only need to come up with a name for your grandmother, but I bet she would like grandma. Try it out when you see her."

Noah gazed around the room slowly taking it all in then turned to Mike and plunged into his arms for a hug…a hug that Mike had been waiting weeks for.

$$\oint$$

After a bunch of smooches and hugs from his Grandma and Mama at the door, Noah headed out with Mike for his first cab ride. Stopping at the bottom of the steps before getting into a taxi at the curb, Noah turned to wave goodbye. Grandma and Mama both looked like they were about to cry.

"Don't be sad. I'm coming back," he said, assuredly.

This caused Naomi to gasp with a sob and his Grandma to throw out her arms and shout, "We'll miss you. Don't be gone too long."

Noah looked up at his father then said, "Okay, we won't."

Mike then scooped him up, tucked him under his arm and hustled to the waiting cab with Noah giggling all the way.

$\flat$

Mike held Noah on his lap in the back seat of the taxi so he could look out at the passing city. As Noah's head rotated around like it was on a swivel, the sun briefly peeked through clouds that forecasted a stormy afternoon. The ride down Fifth Avenue from Harlem past Central Park brought back a myriad of memories for Mike – the emotional debut concert at the Naumberg band shell and the frantic carriage ride in Central Park to try and save Sarah, who was the inspiration for his composition *The Girl in the Yellow Scarf.* But then there were also the romantic picnics with Naomi before they were married.

Mike had tried to call R.G. but no one answered so he decided to go straight to the Y to see if any of the kids might be practicing there.

Pulling up to the entrance, Mike leaned forward to pay the cabby – Noah studying his every move. After getting out, Mike stopped at the curb looking at the entrance in a reverie, thinking of the hours he and Naomi put in to get the Y kids ready for their competition at Radio City Music Hall. *Man, it's good to be back. Can't wait to see those kids.*

Mike led Noah to the reception desk to ask the clerk if any of his students might be there and if not to get the key so he could play the piano for a while. The clerk, finished talking on the phone, got up and came to the counter with his hand out.

"Mike Monroe. You're back in town?"

"Yeah, man, back to stay I hope. Just checking to see if any of my students are here today?"

The clerk's face dropped and he looked away. "Ahhhh…"

"What is it?"

"They were kicked out a few weeks ago after they just about destroyed the room, fighting."

"What?" Mike shouted, drawing his hands to his head.

18

Scattered

Jaz burst into Johnny's muttering curses and went straight to the bathroom. Blake trailed in moments later shaking his head.

From the dark end of the bar that ran the length of the room on the right, Mike watched Blake and Jaz storm into Johnny's. After dropping Noah off in Harlem, he'd been catching up with Rudy but seeing the latest drama unfold in front of him he held out his palms and questioned, "Is this what you've been putting up with?"

"Yeah…pretty much," Rudy said with a snort. "They're almost as bad as you used to be."

Mike glowered at Rudy, but then got he was jiving him and sat back to wait for Jaz to come out of the bathroom.

Blake, mumbling something, went straight to the old baby grand across the room and propped up the lid and sat down. He closed his eyes and warmed up with a number Mike hadn't heard before. Rudy leaned on the bar to listen then turned to Mike.

"He's almost as good as you. Give him a little time and he'll probably be better."

Mike grunted and let Rudy's friendly jab go without comment. *Damn, this kid is good.* Mike was about to get up when Jaz came down the hall from the bathroom. She scowled at Rudy then squinted in the dimly lit bar. Seeing Mike, she stopped in her tracks. She dropped her head and ambled up and stood silently in front of him.

Mike swallowed the urge to question what was going on; instead slid off his stool to give her a hug. Her arms dangled at her sides.

Jaz, softened with a sigh, leaned back and looked up at him. "When'd you get back?"

"Just this morning. Couldn't wait to see you guys."

Blake, finally realizing it was Mike at the bar, wove his way through the scattering of tables and chairs with his hand out.

"Oh man…it's so good to see you. You home for awhile?"

Mike shook Blake's hand then pulled him in for a quick hug.

"I am. But looks like I won't be getting my old job back. You sound pretty good."

Blake gave Jaz a quick glance. "Thanks."

Rudy coughed to get Blake's attention and nodded toward the piano. The place was beginning to fill with couples out on date night.

Mike watched his young protégés make their way back to the piano. Jaz glanced over her shoulder at him on her way. Mike smiled with not a little pride but knew there was a storm brewing just beneath the surface. He would wait until their break to find out what happened at the Y but for now tried to relax and figure how he would round up the remains of *La Familia de Musica.*

𝄞

Mia looked out her bedroom window above the family restaurant and began to whimper. She had to face that she wasn't going to Julliard, at least not for another year or so. Being the oldest in a family of five kids, she had been trained to take over managing the restaurant while her mother, diagnosed with liver cancer, left with her father for Hong Kong and treatment from the family doctor they hoped would save her mother's life. Mia fought not to be angry and often hid out in her room so they wouldn't see her increasing melancholy. She owed them everything but could hardly contain her disappointment. Now, after the fight at the practice room at the Y, she didn't even have her friends in the band to hang out with.

𝄞

"Abby dear," Nana shouted from outside her granddaughter's bedroom. "You aren't going to make your class tonight if you don't get going."

Abby's grandmother kept the apartment on the Upper West Side in Manhattan mainly so her granddaughter would have a safe place to stay while going to NYU until she could audition for either MSM or Julliard in the spring. The oceanfront estate in South Hampton was closed for the winter.

After a long moment of silence Nana opened the door to an empty room. She walked in, looked around, then saw a note on Abby's bed.

Anxiety shot through her like an electric shock as she moved to pick it up. She stood over Abby's empty bed gripping the note like it might portend someone's death.

Dearest Nana,

Please don't be angry but I just need to take a break from everything and think about what I really want to do with my life before I commit to years at college. I'll be okay and Cobi and I have enough to live on for at least a month until we find work. I'll write often to let you know where we are, but for now we're headed to L.A.

Please trust me, and don't worry.

Love you, Abby

Nana staggered back to sit in Abby's desk chair that overlooked Central Park. *How could this happen? And why Cobi?*

Carlos's dad, just home from work, answered the front door. "Hey, Tobias. Carlos isn't home but I bet you know where he is."

Tobias huffed. "Let me guess…Sofia?"

His dad nodded with a slight frown. "Want to come in for a bit? Said they would be back in a little while."

"Nah. I got stuff to do. I'll catch up with him later."

"Sorry, son. Honestly, I'm not all that excited about his choice."

Tobias snarled. "Yeah. Me neither."

He turned in disgust and bound down the porch steps, muttering. "Guess it's time to find another bass player."

Mike was impressed by the crowd's reaction to Blake, Albert and Jaz. Regardless of their earlier huff, they connected with the audience like pros, challenging each other to improvise yet blending for a fresh rendition of an old standard or pop song. Mike was pleased but frustrated thinking they could easily get stuck the way he had, pounding out nightly gigs; blue-collar musicians. It could be a good living but sensed these two would need something more.

When the applause died down at the end of their set, Jaz's face returned to its usual edge as she headed for the restroom. Seeing Mike, her face softened and she redirected her steps toward him. Not saying a word she reached out for a hug. He reached for her before he could stand up. He felt a fatherly affection for this tightly wound teenager – still a child trying to appear tough. Mike had seen it before; kids not knowing who they should become – having lost a parent or never knowing them.

Mike held her out. "You sound amazing, Jaz. I can see how much this means to you – and the crowd loves you."

She gazed at the floor, her eyes reddening. "Hope you never leave again."

Mike swallowed hard.

Blake came over and Rudy set out a couple cokes. Mike nodded to an empty table in the corner and they followed him over.

Mike sat across from them trying to muster some optimism. "Heard there was a bit of a row at the Y and you've been evicted."

Blake turned and puckered his lips. Jaz cocked her head and peered at Blake.

"What happened?" Mike asked.

Blake drew in a long breath. "It was a mess."

"Yes?" Mike said.

Blake peered at Jaz. "Cobi knocked Jaz into the piano. When I saw the cut in her head I got into it with him. Then Carlos and Tobias got involved."

Mike frowned. "Why would Cobi go after Jaz?"

"She kind of knocked Abby down by accident and Cobi charged in playing the big hero."

Mike wondered how so much could have changed in only three months.

"You guys still getting together to play?"

"Ha…don't think so. Haven't seen any of them in weeks," Jaz replied.

Mike held up his hands. "Okay. Okay. What about R.G? Have you gotten over to work with him?"

Jaz looked like she wanted to hold back information. "He's not real happy with us either, I guess…and he didn't look all that great the last time I saw him."

Mike felt guilty for not connecting with R.G. as soon as he got back. "What do you mean?"

Jaz's face fell. "He looked sick."

"What? Haven't you been checking in with him?"

Jaz peered down at the table and shook her head.

"And what about you, Blake?"

He began to say something –.

"What the hell, you guys! You're supposed to be looking after each other. Shit!"

Mike sprung from his seat and went to the bar – steaming. Rudy saw him and came over.

"You don't look happy," Rudy said.

Mike peered up at him, his mouth stretched in a line.

"Mike, for God's sake, they're still kids."

Mike looked over his shoulder at them, moaned and shook his head.

19
Reality Check

Early Sunday before the rest of the family members were up, Naomi stared across the breakfast table, wondering how to get Mike out of his funk. She sat patiently as he told her about the fight at the Y and how he still couldn't locate R.G. – hearing he was sick. His neighbors only knew they hadn't seen him in the hall for a couple of days.

"Mike...I'm so sorry I dragged you to Liberia. This is all my fault."

He seemed to snap out from a bad dream and gazed at her, sad eyed. "It's not your fault at all. How can I expect to save the kids from struggling? Look how long I had to stumble around."

She reached to hold his hands. "You haven't lost them, Mike. They love you."

He looked away – mute.

She squeezed his hands to get his attention. "Now then...we have a challenge of our own. Getting Noah into school and deciding which grade. I'll get an appointment at PS 177 tomorrow for starters." She paused to search his eyes. "Any thoughts?"

"Yeah. I don't know if we can just drop him into any old class. And remember he wasn't exactly a model student in Liberia."

Naomi squinted at him, not understanding his negativity. "That's why we need to get some advice from the school."

Mike pulled his hands away and crossed his arms. "Sorry. It's one thing to mentor someone else's kids, but now I'm responsible for his very life and who he will become, keeping him safe –"

"Stop!" Naomi slapped her hand on the table and leaned forward. "You have to remember what kind of life he had."

Mike seemed to get a grip and peered at her. "We didn't adopt him because we wanted to save him from the streets. We wanted that child. Especially not being able to conceive on our own."

Naomi gasped. She brought her hand to her face – dread torn. "Mike, I didn't mean to deceive you. I should have told you before…" she chocked back a sob.

He quickly slid his chair around, sat next to her and held her. "I love you. That doesn't change at all how I feel about you."

Just then Noah bound into the kitchen from the hall and plunged into them – joyful.

Mike burst out in a grin. "Now…look what we've been blessed with."

Naomi swiped away tears from her cheeks. She pulled the sweet child into her lap, hugged and smothered him with kisses.

Soon the rest of the clan sauntered into the kitchen. Jesse went straight for a cup of coffee, then Persis swayed in with her bulging belly. A minute later Trina and Brenda, a friend from college, ambled in, home for the weekend. Rose stopped at the hall doorway with smiling eyes – appraising the gathering.

"Okay gang, I do love you all, but please head to the dining room so I can get you fed before we go to church. But first I need a hug from someone special."

All the adults looked around then pointed to themselves. "No, it's not any of you who think you are so wonderful. This person is the bravest, most handsome and probably the smartest one in the room."

Each of the adults moaned feigning disappointment and hung their heads.

Rose reached out to Noah. "Come here, my beautiful boy." Noah lit up like Fourth of July fireworks and streaked into his grandma's arms.

$$\oint$$

After a Sunday of showing off their son to all the folks at church and a dinner of grandma's special Georgia cooking, Monday was about getting Noah enrolled in school. They got up early and toured three different schools but it was soon apparent which would suit Noah the best. He would need extra help with reading and language, still hanging onto much of his Pidgin English. Having a degree in early education, Naomi understood his needs better than most and was eager to work with her child. She couldn't wait to get started – Noah not so much. Mike sensed Noah's apprehension but understood exactly what he was feeling not having been a great student himself.

Getting back to the house after their meetings Mike was anxious to call R.G. and hunt down more of the kids.

Finally, on the sixth ring, R.G. answered his phone. "Hello."

"R.G., I was afraid you had left town or died. Where you been?"

"Mike?"

"Yeah…sorry. I should have let you know earlier we were coming back. Everything has changed…everything." Mike paused. "Will you be home for awhile? I need to see you about the Y kids."

The phone was silent.

"R.G.…you there?"

"Yeah, Mike. Come over. It's your place after all."

Mike paused, something wasn't right. "I'll grab a cab. Be there soon."

"It'll be good to see ya, Mike," R.G. whispered.

Mike hung up and stared at the phone. He needed to get going but hated to leave his son behind, although Naomi was taking him shopping and Mike hated shopping.

𝄞

Mike got out of the cab and stood at the front of the Greenwich Apartments. He looked up at his fourth floor window, transfixed in a reverie. The parties. The endless hours he put in playing. The night he almost burned down the place. He wondered if he would ever compose again with his responsibilities of family and mentoring. Anxiety crept in but he shook it off needing to see R.G.

It was weird to knock on his old door. "R.G., it's me."

There came scuffling from behind the door and the sound of latches and a sliding bolt. R.G. shuffled back with the door.

What the hell?

Mike tried not to give away his shock and reached to hug his old friend.

"Hey man. It's great to see you."

"You too, Mike," R.G. said and shuddered briefly before going to sit at the kitchen table in the alcove on the right.

Mike pulled his eyes off R.G. to look around at his old apartment. It seemed years not just months since he had lived there. He couldn't help but be drawn to the ebony grand piano, the lid scarred from the fire that almost cost him everything.

"Mind if I play something?"

R.G. looked in Mike's direction and laid his palms on the table. "Mike...please do."

Mike ached to play. But seeing R.G. looking so emaciated broke his heart. He went and sat across from him instead.

"Okay my friend. What's going on with you?"

R.G. sat back and dropped his hands in his lap. After a moment, with his head bowed, he told Mike he just got out of the hospital this morning. It wasn't good news. Stage-four lung cancer – too many nights playing in smoky bars.

How can this be? R.G. was the sweetest person he had ever known. This isn't fair.

After a moment, Mike realized he was holding his breath.

"What can we do? What do you need? Maybe a second opinion? I've got a friend from college who's a doctor. I'll call him and see what he thinks. I would trust his opinion." Mike was beginning to hyperventilate. "We can see you get the best care, man."

R.G. sat silently with his hands in his lap and shook his head.

"What?" Mike said.

R.G. leaned toward Mike. "My brother...it's okay."

"Okay? It's not, OKAY!"

R.G. lifted his chin. "Listen to me. I've come to terms with it. Besides...I'm tired."

Mike was struck – helpless. Another good man was leaving him.

"I don't wanna waste time on what can't be changed, Mike, so let's talk 'bout what's goin' on with you. Couple weeks ago your mama tole me all 'bout the weddin' and you adoptin' a child. Man…things are changin' fast for you. Tell me 'bout this boy."

Reluctantly Mike set aside his concern for R.G. and explained how the adoption came about and the challenges of Noah adjusting to his new life. After catching up on the news about his old band, *The Gathering*, they fell silent.

R.G. puckered his lips and gave a little snort. "Well, s'pose you'd like to hear what's goin' on with your kids."

Mike scrubbed his chin. "Yeah, I was going to get to that. Is there any good news?"

R.G. pulled his hands up and rubbed the back of his neck. "Travis has kept me up to date on their antics. Think he's the only one has his head screwed on right."

R.G. paused as if struck with even greater pain.

"But first, Mike…I'm sorry. I let you down. They've pretty much lost their way. Cobi and Abby left New York to chase a dream in L.A. thinkin' they need to escape their *oppressive* families. Mia, I'm told, had to give up playin' at the Winter Garden Theater to take responsibility for the family restaurant while her parents left for Hong Kong for cancer treatments for her mother."

Mike winced at the sound of cancer again. He closed his eyes and waited for R.G. to continue.

"With Cobi gone, Carlos and Tobias's little band fell apart. Don't know what they're up to now. And you know 'bout Blake and Jaz. Travis says it's just a matter of time before Jaz gets 'em fired. When I stopped in ta Johnny's Rudy was reamin' them pretty good with Jaz being Jaz."

Gloom fell over Mike. What good was all the work getting to Radio City to end up doing stupid stuff? In the end…he had done little to help them. *Crap.*

20
Autumn Leaves - November

Mike's new life as husband and father was challenging to say nothing of what to do about the Y kids. Also, with royalties dwindling, he had to get a grip on his finances and make a plan to find a place to live other than the house he grew up in. He sat in his mother's kitchen staring at his coffee cup, wondering what to do next. Naomi came out from the bedroom down the hall and reached around with a hug.

"Morning, lover. I was hoping we could snuggle a little this morning. But you left me."

Mike looked over his shoulder at her.

"Sorry." Mike moaned. "Seems I'm saying that a lot lately. To be honest I'm a little lost here."

"Here?" Naomi chortled.

"What are you laughing at?"

"It's funny because it's your home and yet I've never felt so secure. I love your family. I see why you turned out so good," she said with a little smirk.

Mike loved seeing her happy, but why was he so unsettled? She pulled his chair back from the table and sat in his lap and held his face.

"What is it, my sweetness?"

Mike looked into her kind chestnut eyes and couldn't help but smile. "I'm so blessed. I have you, Noah, my family…"

"But, your Y children are lost and you haven't done anything creative lately." Naomi paused and peered at him with a laser like gaze. "My dear, I think you're suffering from creativity constipation."

"What? There's no such thing. You're making that up!"

Naomi grinned. "Yeah… I am making it up but I've seen it in you before. When we were working with the kids before the Radio City competition. You needed to do something original, not just play someone else's music. Then in Liberia, you would get cranky if you didn't have time at the piano improvising." Naomi suddenly appeared stern. "Yep, creativity constipation. You don't know that about yourself do you?"

Mike hunched. "Huh…I don't know. Could be right. What do you suggest?"

"I don't know but you'll figure it out."

Mike groaned. "I've done nothing worthwhile without something that stirred me."

Naomi chuckled. "I can think of eight teenagers that could *stir* you. Then there's that beautiful boy that came to us out of the storm."

Mike had put the Y kids out of his mind for a couple days, but began to fantasize about finding something that could draw his renegade bunch back into the fold.

Naomi lifted Mike's chin and burrowed into his brain with a furrowed look that meant he'd better pay attention.

"Persis and I are taking Noah shopping for school clothes. He doesn't have much to keep him warm. Would you like to go with us?" she said in all innocence.

Mike snorted. "You're kidding…right?"

"I take it that's a no?"

Be kind. She doesn't know you hate shopping. "If you don't mind I would like some time to noddle at the piano and give my old agent, Jimmy, a call 'bout finding a gig or two."

"Okay," she said and kissed him on the forehead and left to get Noah ready to leave.

After Mike saw them off in a taxi he found his way to the living room piano and was soon lost in a sketch. Going on an hour, he sensed someone was in the room with him. He slid around to find his mother in her favorite chair with her hands to her face – faintly smiling.

"How long have you been there?"

"Long enough to know you better get that down before you lose it. That's new isn't it?"

Mike nodded.

"What's the inspiration?"

Mike looked out the window then down at the keyboard. "The eternal question. What's really important in this life? But I wonder sometimes if making music really has any lasting value."

"Oh my." His mother leaned back and studied him a moment. "What's going on? Surely you're not questioning if what you're doing with the Y kids is valuable?"

His mother stood, walked up to him and put her hands on his shoulders. "Don't doubt yourself. You're doing right by those kids."

Mike looked up with a crooked smile. "Maybe."

She reached for his hand and led him to the couch.

"I need to bring you up to date on what's going on with the Reverend and me."

𝄞

Mike was sitting on the back porch thinking he needed to get at raking the leaves piling up, when Naomi walked in with Noah wearing a huge grin.

"Wow! Who is this young man?" Mike said, reaching out as Noah plunged into him.

"You like my new threads, Papa?"

"Threads?" Mike questioned with a grin, looking up at Naomi.

"The young salesman had some fun with Noah."

"I see. What else do you have in that bag?"

Mike got to see the whole wardrobe that ranged from shorts, jeans and Nikes to church clothes: navy-blue pants, white shirts, tie and black oxfords – Noah oblivious to the uncool factor of "church-clothes".

After Noah rushed off to change into his play clothes and head outside, Naomi slid in next to Mike on the loveseat that looked out onto the yard.

"Okay. What is it now?"

Mike pulled back and squinted at her. "What is it with you women? Mother asked me the same question."

Naomi simply raised her eyebrows and waited.

"Mother imparted some interesting news a while ago. Seems her and the Reverend are thinking of getting married."

"Oh really," Naomi said, *acting* surprised.

"Yeah…so you knew already."

"Not exactly, but all the signs were there," she said, shimmering with anticipation. "So fill me in on the details."

"The wedding is one thing but she's thinking of selling the house and moving to his place," Mike said looking off into the yard.

"Oh…" Naomi moaned.

"Being such close friends with my dad, I think the Reverend would feel awkward moving here."

Now Naomi looked out the window at the autumn leaves tumbling across the yard.

21
Family Meeting

After a couple weeks settling in at his mother's, Mike decided it was time to call a family meeting, something they hadn't done since his father died. As a kid their meetings were usually about making plans for a vacation or a party or discussing and assigning chores around the house. But this would be different. He needed help with some life decisions. He had his kid sister Trina come down from Cornell for the weekend and connected with Persis and Jesse to bring food from the store deli and bakery so Mother wouldn't have to cook. Mike sat at the head of the dinning room table, gazing around at the gathering with a raging river of emotions.

"Sorry. I don't mean to appear overly dramatic. But, with all that's happening lately, and with everyone so busy, it seemed best to meet all at once. Besides, I think it is a good idea to establish regular family meetings with my own family like we used to do." Mike glanced over at Naomi holding Noah in her lap.

Mike continued. "Like before, we'll go around the table so everyone can share what's going on with them and share their opinions on what we discuss. And, as I remember, no one ever held back on their sentiments."

Jesse feebly raised his hand. "Can we eat first? I missed breakfast because your sister didn't set the alarm and I had to run off to my publisher without a bite."

Mike moaned and scrunched his face.

Jesse hunched with a pleading look.

"Okay," Mike said raising his hands. "I don't know if alarm clock setting is worthy of discussion time, but I guess we can continue meeting while we eat."

Mike missed his dad at times like this. He had a knack for engaging everyone that Mike seemed to lack.

When everyone was back at the table with their food, Trina started the conversation by saying she hoped to go to her roommate's home in Vermont over Christmas. This got positive vibes from everyone except Mother who didn't object but didn't exactly smile about it either.

"Well, we won't be going anywhere," Persis said, rubbing her belly. "But Jesse's parents might fly over after the baby comes. Looking more and more like Christmas."

"A Christmas baby…" Mother said, then sniffled.

Persis leveled an eye at Mike before he got out a comment about poor planning – recalling there wasn't any planning. Mike turned his smirk aside and continued as meeting chairman.

"Mother. Any news on your plans for the future?" Mike said, peering at her through his eyebrows.

His mother went on to explain that she and James (Reverend Robinson) had agreed on a date in March to get married and would be moving into a smaller apartment soon after. She heaved a great sigh, looked around then off into the living room as if recalling something bittersweet.

Mike knew this was coming so had rehearsed with Naomi and Noah to sing *Oh Happy Day* at the piano along with a little choreography. They had just got started when the rest of the family got up and ran to join in a line dance that Trina lead from the piano around to the dining room table and back. Mike was unexpectedly struck with conflicting emotions – at first happy, then sad. He briefly closed his eyes. *Love you, Dad.*

When the impromptu celebration had calmed down, Trina, with her best smarty pants look, said, "Now…how about you, Mikey? Anything going on in your world, now that you've settled down and become an old married man?"

Mike had a brief vision of torturing her with a noogie until she cried uncle, like when they were kids…but just snorted instead.

"Yeah, we do have something to run by you all." Mike gazed at Naomi and Noah and puckered his lips. "We're thinking about going into business."

Persis just about lost it. "You *have* to be kidding. You hated the idea of running the stores."

Mike hunched his shoulders. "Well…a guy can change his mind."

Mike could hardly understand it himself. Six months ago if someone suggested he start a business he would've laughed himself silly. However, Naomi seemed to have an understanding that was lost to him. When she intuited that his mother would be getting married soon Naomi suggested they needed to find their own place. That made sense, but what was really brilliant was that the apartment advertised in Chelsea also had a small bookshop beneath it that was available. Why a bookshop? To possibly change it into a café/coffeehouse; one that could bring in a little income and serve as a home base for young musicians to practice and perform, especially his renegade Y students.

"Sounds like the bookstore owner has been looking to sell for over a year and is anxious to unload it." Mike paused and looked at his family – his face twisted. "So what do you think? Are we nuts?"

Persis leaned back and flashed Mike her big sister look. "Either of you good with finances and keeping books?" She then directed her gaze to Naomi. "Actually, I know Mike's answer to that."

Naomi gave Mike a sideward glance with raised eyebrows.

Trina quickly chimed in. "Café? You mean like…with food and drinks?"

Mike cocked his head and puffed his cheeks. "Sure, why not?" Then caught Trina's eye-roll.

After a moment of dead silence, Jesse spoke up. "I think your heart's in the right place…but you both are artists. This sounds like a business decision."

Mother broke in after another moment of quiet. "Mike, you studied business for awhile at Cornell. I'll bet you could do this if you put your mind to it."

Mike cringed.

Mother then looked at Persis briefly and was about to say something then changed her mind. "Maybe you could hire a manager for awhile to get it up and running."

Mike nodded. "Like I said, it's a thought. We're just going to check out the apartment for now."

A bit deflated from the cool reaction, Mike changed the subject and asked Jesse how his writing was going.

Jesse sat a moment with his head down then looked up and gazed around at his new family. "I recently had an unusual story push its way into my thoughts that is a result from joining this...ah...this amazing family." He stopped to let this settle over the table.

Mother tipped her head and peered at him. "Jesse, dear. I'm not sure I like being the subject of a novel. Can you elaborate a little?"

The corner of Jesse mouth twitched slightly and he said in all seriousness, "Oh, don't worry, I'll change your names. Just tell me what you would like to be called."

Mother lowered her head and gave Jesse "the look".

"Just kidding," he said quickly. "Really...it's more about the idea of the journey we all are on." Jesse paused to collect his thoughts. "You all have enriched my life, helping me understand what everyone has in common." He paused. "I mean look at me. I've been a sheltered kid from the mid-west most of my life, writing stories from the inside out. But I've gained insight into what we all have in common through moving here and joining this family. This is a powerful theme to me and I want to explore it. I've been searching for my story core for a while and think I've found it."

Mike reached across the table with his palm up for some skin from Jesse...thinking; *thank God he's got Persis to keep his feet on the ground.*

"Okay, Runt. Anything else besides going to Vermont for Christmas and gaining weight from all that dorm food?"

Trina spoke up, ignoring Mike's lame little joke. "Actually, my roommate from LA is driving me nuts with her valley talk. And the other one, from a Reservation in Arizona, who's so quiet I haven't a clue what she's thinking."

Mike snorted. "You've been there what? A couple weeks now? Give it some time. Bet you seem alien to them, too."

Trina nodded and let a slight grin escape. "I suppose."

Naomi then brought up how she was keeping in touch with the orphanage in Liberia and thinking of ways to raise money to help rebuild the school destroyed in the September storm. This brought about a lively discussion, with Naomi noting suggestions – bake sales, selling Liberian craft items and possibly a benefit concert at Harlem Baptist Church.

Mike sat back, his heart warmed – seeing his family all together. Something he had been craving without realizing it until now. However, on to more immediate issues – making a living to support his new family. *But will opening a café make enough? And what about his creative constipation?*

22

Entrepreneur?

Mike lay in bed staring at the ceiling, Naomi tucked into him hugging his arm. It was going on midnight. He needed to talk.

"You asleep?" he asked, looking down at his bride.

Naomi moaned. "Sort of."

"Not a great reception to our idea." Mike puffed his cheeks. "Persis pretty much thought we were crazy. But she knows what it takes and…" Mike groaned. "I don't know."

Naomi sleepily reached up and wove her fingers in his hair. "Let's go to Chelsea after church and see what our hearts tell us. I believe things will fall into place if it's meant to be."

Mike groaned again.

Naomi rubbed the back of his neck. "If you think about it, you have a number of people that could help. Along with your sister Persis, there's Rudy, Al who manages the soup kitchen and even Leo from the donut shop. Don't think you have to figure this out by yourself."

Mike squeezed his eyes shut and sighed. He wished he could just make music and mentor the Y kids.

𝄞

Mike watched his mother hover over Noah, making sure his every need was met. *She's going to spoil this boy, terribly. Good thing there'll be another grandchild soon.*

"Think you'll be able to handle this boy while we're gone to Chelsea?" Mike asked, reaching to toss down the last of his coffee.

"After you…I think I can *handle* anything." Mother paused and winked at Noah looking up at her.

"When we're done looking at the apartment, I might check in with my agent Jimmy to see if he can scare up some work." Mike tightened, trying not to let on his concern. But nothing much gets past his mother.

"Michael, take all the time you need." She said, nodding to let him know she understood how he was feeling.

"Do we have time to stop in to see Rudy? He might have some thoughts on running a cafe," Naomi said.

"Sure." Mike bobbed his head. "Mother, we might be late. Positive you can handle this child?"

Rose just rolled her eyes and shook her head in the direction of the door.

𝄞

Mike debated what to say to Naomi as she nestled in close on the taxi ride to Chelsea. But he'd learned it was wise to keep her abreast of things that bothered him.

Heading down Central Park West, amidst a swarm of yellow taxis, Mike started with, "Ahhh…" when their cab stopped at a traffic light at 72nd Street. As he turned to look out the window in thought, the Dakota apartment building came into view – bringing to mind the tragic death of John Lennon and The Beatles song *Let It Be.*

"You want to…say something?" Naomi questioned.

Mike put on a face he hoped wouldn't betray the acid eating a hole in his gut.

"The royalties from all things connected with *The Girl* are dropping off…rapidly. We've got less than twenty grand saved after all the hype about explosive record sales and I haven't a clue where our next dollar's coming from. I don't know how we can think of buying anything at this time."

Naomi peered up at him and studied his face until he looked down at her.

"How many times have you moved ahead not knowing how things would turn out?"

Mike didn't need much time to reflect. "Too often I'm afraid."

"So," she puzzled. "What's in the way now?"

"You're kidding right," he snapped back.

Naomi scrunched her forehead. "What?"

"It's not just me anymore, is it?"

Naomi pulled back, appearing hurt. "Mike, I'm not asking you to change. If you start giving up on your dreams for us you won't be the person I fell in love with."

Mike considered this.

"I'm here to support you not stifle you. I was hoping you could trust me to help with decisions."

Mike scrubbed his forehead. "Sorry. I'll try to include you. Besides, if we screw up you get to share in the blame." Mike brightened. "That would be great!"

Naomi snuffled. "I get an equal vote you know."

Mike's eyes bulged wide and feigned surprise. "Now you tell me," he said, holding her gaze. But then gave in to her sweet spirit and tilted to kiss her forehead but she met him with her soft full lips. Heat suddenly swept between them.

Mike wiggled his eyebrows. "Maybe we should consider staying the night somewhere. I'm sure Mother would love it. We could call it the honeymoon we never had."

"Ooh," she said. "That would be naughty."

"I hope so." Mike chuckled. "I'll call Mother then the landlord at the apartment to tell him something came up and we'll meet with him tomorrow."

"I don't know. Would your mother approve?"

Mike reached for her left hand and raised it in front of her. "You do remember we're married?"

Naomi twisted her hand back and forth to admire her wedding ring. "Ooh yeah. I almost forgot about that," she said and grabbed his face with both hands for a kiss.

♪

Mike woke with Naomi snuggled next to him at the Gramercy Hotel. Before checking in they shopped at Macy's for a fresh change of clothes for today. The rooms had seen better days but were reasonable. There was talk of making it into a five star hotel but Mike had his doubts.

Mike rolled over and nuzzled Naomi's neck. She scrunched her shoulder and giggled.

"Suppose we should get going before we end up staying another night," she simpered.

Mike rolled on his back and groaned. "I suppose. But I kind of like the idea of spreading out our honeymoon – maybe over the next year or so. What do you think?"

"I'm sure your mother wouldn't mind. But for now shouldn't we check in with Rudy and the landlord? I think that was the plan…right?"

"Ah, reality. But first how bout some room service and…?"

Naomi grinned. "You first."

𝄞

After a late breakfast they stopped in at Johnny's a couple of blocks away, hoping to catch Rudy who often came in for the lunch crowd. Not seeing him anywhere, after heading in to the dark cavernous club, Mike went straight to the baby grand sitting out from the wall on the left. He sat down and looked up and down the keyboard. A deep reverie enveloped him, Naomi peering down from a stool next to him.

"How can I possibly miss something that was often so contentious? Rudy should have fired me a half-dozen times."

"My Dear," her voice mimicking that of a great sage. "All the difficult times help make us who we are. And I love how you're turning out. Another fifty years and you'll be perfect."

Mike peered up scowling but couldn't hold it and grinned.

"Okay…what would you like to hear, smarty pants?"

"Do you know *Bridge Over Troubled Water*?"

"No…but I could fake it. In Garfunkel's E-flat version or the slower Roberta Flack cover?"

Naomi puffed. "*You're* the smarty pants. Nice and slow like Roberta Flack."

Mike straightened at the piano appearing formal like he was about to perform at Carnegie Hall and began with the intro – nice and slow.

As Naomi began to sing she was also trying not to laugh. But, when she came to the end of the song, Mike looked up at her. She was not smiling. Her eyes were wet with tears. He caught his breath – struck by her love message. *I don't deserve her.*

Holding the last chord with his left hand, Mike reached out to her. Naomi slid off the stool – sat on the bench and kissed him. The two regulars at the end of the bar clapped softly as Rudy headed out toward them from behind the bar.

"You're hired. When can you start?"

After pointing out the pitfalls of running a business, Rudy realized they were serious and agreed to mentor them. But as they headed out to meet the landlord in Chelsea, Rudy cast an exaggerated smile and salutation, "You two will always have work here...if it doesn't work out." Mike wasn't sure how to take that.

Approaching the bookshop on 8th Avenue, with Naomi in hand, Mike was immediately smitten by the warm glow of the interior coming through the black-framed multi-paned bay window. The entrance, a red framed door to the left – gave the appearance of a shop that could have been in a cozy English village. Mike stopped with Naomi to take it in. The shop couldn't have been more than about fifty feet wide – with a hunter green awning – charming came to mind.

They decided to check out the apartment first and entered through a door on the right. When they reached the second floor landing, the apartment door was already open. Chilled from their walk from Johnny's they were drawn to sunlight streaming in from the large window on the left facing the street. The market across the street would be handy and the subway was only a block away. Appraising the view, still holding hands like teenagers, they turned to gaze around the room. The living room ceiling was two stories high with an open stairway on the left that led to a landing and two loft bedrooms. They turned to face each other with wow in their eyes but tried to appear nonchalant for the landlord.

"Interesting," Mike said. "Has there been any structural issues with the loft?" trying to come up with something his father might have asked.

The landlord got a little twinkle in his eye. "Oh…I think it'll hold. It's been there for over half a century."

"Good…" Mike replied.

After checking out the half-century kitchenette and equally ancient bathroom and laundry, they were led up the stairs to the two bedrooms. Reaching the landing Mike instinctively tested the railing for strength – it didn't budge. Looking down onto the living room below then out the windows facing the street he took in a long slow breath. The openness reminded him of the landing overlooking the foyer in his parent's home in Harlem. He always loved sitting up there as a kid to spy on his sister's date or daydream out the front living room windows. He was sure Noah would love the view.

He could tell Naomi wasn't too pleased about the grubby condition of the bedrooms but with some *serious* repair, scrubbing and painting they could be salvaged.

As they were heading out of the bedroom that would be Noah's, Mike spotted a door in the back corner.

"Does that lead to an attic?" He asked, pointing to the door.

The landlord raised his brow. "Yes, but its hardly inhabitable now. Some artist lived there in the 20's but they said he was found dead – frozen."

Naomi's eyes grew big, but before she could get a word out the landlord continued.

"Sorry…that's a myth. The artist simply disappeared one day, the paintings he left behind were sold off for back rent and it was never lived in again."

When the tour of the apartment and bookshop was complete, the three of them sat in the small back office of the store with the landlord sitting back in an ancient swivel chair, his feet up on the desk.

"Sorry, guys...but I'm bushed. Any thoughts on what you've seen here?"

"Oh...about a hundred. We'll have to talk it over. But we've got one for sure. You think there would be any problem turning the store into a coffeehouse? Thinking we'd like to change things up a bit."

The landlord snorted and stretched his head side to side. "Don't think so. This place has seen a dozen different businesses come and go. Believe it was a restaurant at least twice."

Mike got a jolt of adrenaline he hadn't felt since Naomi first sat next to him at the piano – and played impromptu. *Could this turn out to be as good as that?*

23
Kids

Venice Beach, CA

"Sorry, Cobi," Abby whispered. "I guess this isn't what you expected."

Cobi shook his head. "Yeah...not exactly."

The two of them sat on the tiny patio of their tiny beachfront rental. Skateboarders breezed by – a backdrop of beach volleyball and surfers bobbing on ocean swells further out.

"Well, got a nice tan anyway," quipped Cobi.

Abby moaned. "Sorry, I just don't fit in here. Everyone seems to be just hanging out."

"Wasn't that the idea?"

"Maybe for you." Abby closed her eyes. "Sorry..."

Cobi grunted. "Please. Stop saying that."

Abby sprang up and headed for the water then remembered how freezing cold it was compared to the ocean in front of her grandma's estate in South Hampton. When she got to the lapping waves she turned and started walking along the water's edge in the wet sand.

"Hey! Wait up!" Cobi shouted, running up to her.

Abby kept strolling, looking down at her feet.

"I'm the one who needs to apologize. I should have known better than to trust my half-baked cousin to find us work." Cobi dropped his head to watch his feet sink in the sand with each step.

Abby hated giving up on their plan. Cobi really thought his cousin had connections in the movie industry. 'Studio musicians are in constant demand,' he had said. In reality his cousin had a friend who had a friend who played on a sound track for an obscure martial arts movie. She hadn't heard the whole story until after a week of hunting for the guy and never finding him. This was new for Abby. She had never failed at anything – ever.

Abby veered away from the water and sat in the sand with her head slumped. She aimlessly sketched in the sand with her finger wanting to cry but wouldn't allow it.

Cobi dropped down next to her and leaned into her. "What do you want to do?"

"What am I going to tell people…my parents? This is the stupidest thing I've ever done…by light years."

Cobi was silent for a moment. "This isn't even close to the stupidest thing I've ever done. One time when I was seven I jumped off my grandmother's porch and tried to fly, flapping my arms like mad with cardboard wings taped on. I broke my arm and knocked out a tooth. But I did miss some school so it wasn't so bad."

Abby slowly turned her head to peer at Cobi and rolled her eyes. He presented her with a goofy grin that caused her to slowly lose her grip on her humiliation. She started with a snort. Then convulsed into a mixture of half laughing half crying.

Cobi put his arm around her, not sure if he should console or laugh with her.

𝄞

Chinatown, Manhattan

Travis stopped in to see Mia on his way to play the evening performance at the Winter Garden Theater. He was concerned because she hadn't returned his phone calls after she had to quit the pit orchestra at the theater. He slipped into a booth at her parents' Chinese restaurant seeing her busy seating a large group in the back.

"Hey," Travis said from the corner of his booth when Mia walked past him.

Mia turned to him appearing stoic. "Travis…"

"Can you sit a minute?" he pleaded.

"It's going to get busy," she said looking out at the street.

"Did you know Mr. M is back?"

Mia gasped and brought her hands to her face, her eyes wide – filling with tears.

𝄞

Johnny's

Honey stopped to hand out cokes when the trio took their break.

"Have you seen Mike lately?" Honey asked Jaz.

Jaz took a slug of her drink as Albert and Blake headed out for some fresh air. "Nah. Sure he's busy with his new life now that he's married and has a kid."

"I suppose," Honey offered. "Anyway, the suit at the bar has been checking you out all night, but I think he's harmless."

"Yeah, he dropped a ten spot in the tip jar earlier."

"You guys really are amazing, you know." Honey paused appearing serious. "Rudy's lucky to have you."

A slight smile snuck up on Jaz. "Thanks. Maybe it's time for a raise?"

"Ha!...good luck with that," Honey bellowed and spun around for the bar cackling.

When the boys came in from their break, Jaz was heading back from the bathroom. The suit, sitting at the bar, reached for her arm.

"Hey, girl, love your singing. And you're really looking good tonight."

Jaz came to a halt and looked down at his hand clutching her arm. She turned to face him, deadpan, and slowly peeled away his fingers. She simmered. "Don't touch me."

The suit reached for her shoulder with his other hand. "Hey cocoa puff I was just – " but before he could finish Jaz wheeled around with her clenched little fist clipping him on the chin.

"What the hell?" he screamed and grabbed her with both hands. Blake, in an effort to help Jaz, got up and crashed through the tables, tripping over a chair landing hard – cracking his head and twisting his wrist. Albert was also headed to the action when Rudy scrambled over the bar knocking off glasses and bottles. He grabbed the suit, spun him around and shoved his gut against the bar – wrenching his arm up his back with a jerk.

"Time for you to leave, my friend," Rudy grunted, then escorted the suit – dancing on his toes – to the entrance. Rudy let go of his arm and opened the door for him. "Don't come back until you can act like a gentleman."

The suit sneered at Rudy and stumbled out.

Johnny's was dead silent as Rudy strode back through gaping customers and stood in front of Jaz. "You okay?"

Stunned by the way Rudy handled things, Jaz's heart was still pounding. "Yeah."

"Nice hook you got there, but I'd rather you let me take care of the jerks next time."

Jaz nodded.

"Better check on your piano player. Looks like the chair took him out."

Jaz turned to see Blake bent over rubbing his wrist, a goose egg forming on his forehead. Albert was helping Honey clean up the mess that Blake made charging through the tables.

Jaz strolled over to Blake. "Thanks for trying to help...." She paused, puffing her cheeks in an effort to hold back a guffaw.

"That was sweet," she purred and gave the bump on his head a kiss.

Mike woke early the next morning in a great mood – after their short "honeymoon" at the Gramercy Hotel and checking out the bookstore. He hadn't felt so alive since, well…maybe never. *What should I do first?*

Naomi rolled over to face him and moaned. "What's up? You're all twitchy."

Mike smiled like he just got word they had won the lottery.

"I think I have an idea that will enable us to buy the shop along with the apartment."

Naomi propped herself up on her elbows and squinted at him.

Mike gazed off like he'd received a message from the Almighty.

"Okay…you going to let me in on it?"

"Sure," and paused for dramatic effect. "My agent, Jimmy, has been after me to get the old band together and tour jazz clubs around the country. He feels we still have a following and thinks we could pack the clubs and a few indoor arenas. We could play a lot of the old stuff along with a couple new numbers."

Naomi now scooted up to a full sitting position. "You think you can get everyone together? And is it worth it?"

"It's only a month tour but Jimmy is sure we could come away with about twenty-five grand each. Can't do that good in six months anywhere else. I still have to check with everyone, but I think they're all still in town."

"What about Liz?"

"What do you mean? We need her, too. She's our lead singer."

"Do you think I can trust her?" With a sight sneer, Naomi narrowed her eyes.

"You're joking, right?"

Naomi kept her gaze on him.

"Well…you can certainly trust me can't you?"

Naomi grinned. "Just giving you a little poke."

"Oh yeah…that's real funny," Mike snarled, feigning righteous indignation.

Naomi pouted. "Sorry. Anything I can do to get you to smile?"

Mike crossed his arms. "Maybe."

She uncrossed his arms and wrapped them around her. "I thought there might be."

$\oint$

Mike burst through the kitchen door humming *Here Comes the Sun* – his arms slowly swinging to the beat.

"My Lord!" His mother shouted turning from the kitchen sink, a dishtowel in her hand. "Michael…you're going to give me a stroke yet."

Mike slid up to her with his arms out and gave her a monster hug – swaying side to side to the song in his head.

"Things are lookin' up, Mother. Think I figured how we can get a down payment for the apartment and bookshop."

She leaned back with her arms pinned to her sides and tried to smile. "That's nice, son, but you have to let me go if you want any breakfast."

Mike released her, grinning like a crazy person and plopped down at the table. As he unpacked his plan, his mother tenderly served him – a shadow of melancholy knowing their time living under the same roof was soon coming to an end.

𝄞

Mike sat making calls at his mother's roll top desk in the living room. Everyone he contacted was up for the idea except two, but he figured he could find a replacement for trumpet and violin. *But, what to do about R.G.?* He needed to get over there to see how he was doing.

Mike braced himself as he stood at the door of his old flat and knocked. "Hey, R.G. it's Mike."

𝄞

Mike dragged himself home – defeated. Naomi came into the living room and saw Mike slumped at the piano. She came up behind him.

"Sweetie, you alright?" she asked and slid next to him – putting her arm around him.

"Looks like I've got the musicians I need but there's no way R.G. can do it. He's in pretty bad shape."

Naomi put her head on his shoulder. "I'm sorry. Can anything be done for him?"

Mike moaned. "I don't know…but I've got to do something. Can't stand that he's all alone."

Naomi pulled his chin toward her. "Maybe he could stay here for awhile? You might ask your mother."

Mike heaved a sigh. "I know she loves R.G. I'll see what she thinks when she gets home and check with my old roommate, Frankie, who's a doctor now."

Then he was struck with another thought. "And maybe pass the hat to others in the business for his medical expenses." Mike gazed at his bride. "Thanks for the idea. Least he'll know he's loved."

Mike returned to the phone to reach Franklin and then to contact musicians he knew in the city to help out one of their own.

$$\text{\textit{\large ♪}}$$

Mike was in need of a little joy so he went up to his old bedroom to see his son. When he swung open the door he was immediately slammed with a hug around his waist.

Seeing Lego bricks spread out on the floor, he asked, "What're you building?"

"A tree house for my friends," Noah said looking up with pride.

"Friends? Who are these people?"

"Guys I played wid in Africa."

"Okay," Mike pondered that a beat then continued. "You know...I was wondering if you have time to go shopping... for a soccer ball?" Wrestling was Mike's sport in school but he noticed Noah was surprisingly skilled with the ball – the little they played together in Liberia.

Noah lit up, shaking his head frantically up and down.

"I'll take it that's a yes," Mike laughed and scooping up his son headed downstairs for the door.

After getting back with a shiny new ball, even though chilly at fifty degrees, they set up goals with empty milk cartons on the small patch of grass in the back yard. Playing one-on-one,

Noah easily won the best of three games. Mike found he was definitely out of shape, even running at half speed.

"Okay, hot shot, let's see how good you are at wrestling," Mike said, with his chest puffed up looking down at his skinny son.

"I never wrestle before," Noah replied, peering up with a crooked grin.

"Good!" Mike cried, trying hard to look serious. "Maybe I'll have a chance at winning."

Mike started with some of the basics: A proper stance, simple takedowns and pinning techniques. But after five minutes of fundamentals the rest of the time was spent with Mike on his knees fighting off a ferocious Kung Fu street fighter with gritted teeth – causing Mike to practically hemorrhage from trying not to laugh at his grunting opponent.

With sweat dripping down their faces, Mike – flat on his back with Noah astride his chest – finally gave up and yelled, "Uncle!"

"Uncle?" Noah paused from cranking on Mike's arm. "What you mean?"

"You win, you win! I can't take anymore."

Noah took in a great gulp of air and peered down at him with great pride.

Mike's heart swelled from the love he saw in his child's face. He grabbed his boy and hugged him, rocking side to side. Mike would never be the same man.

♪

When Mike walked in from the back yard, with Noah on his shoulders, Persis, Jesse and his mother had just brought in two large pizzas and were setting the dining room table.

"Pizza? In this house?" Mike questioned, looking at Persis.

"You can thank Jesse. He convinced Mother it would give her a break from cooking," Persis said, giving Mike a crooked smile.

"What the heck! I've been trying to get pizza in this house my whole life," Mike said, pouting.

"Next time you want something just let me know," Jesse said with an angelic air.

Mother slowly turned her head in Jesse's direction with *the look*. "Careful there."

Jesse straightened – fighting a grin. "Just kidding…Mother."

When the pizza was gone except for bits of chewed crust, Noah wormed his way onto Mike's lap and leaned against his chest.

Mike held Noah's smiling face and turned it to his mother. "See what pizza does for this boy. Have you ever seen such contentment?"

"I don't think it's the pizza," Mother said, smiling back.

$$\text{\clef}$$

Mike was speechless. His lap was empty. He had just told his family he'd be leaving in a couple of weeks for a month on tour. It would be grueling but he was thankful for the work. The adults seemed happy, knowing the money would enable them to get the apartment and bookshop. But Noah had appeared stricken. He'd inched off Mike's lap and run up to his room – sobbing.

A slash of bitter wind wiped at Travis's trench coat and scarf as he stood at the window of the Hong Kong Garden Restaurant – hoping to catch a glimpse of Mia. Of course she's there. She's always there. When she saw him peering in through the window she beamed. He was feeling pretty down, but that smile...

Mia walked up to him after he entered and gave him a hug without hesitation, catching him off guard. A flash of warmth rose up from his collar.

"Good to see you, Travis," she said, looking up at him – a touch of spring.

"Got a minute?" he murmured.

Mia nodded in the direction of a booth in the back corner.

"Want a bite to eat? Something to drink?" she asked after they sat down, facing each other.

Travis shook his head. "No, I'm good."

Mia studied him – her head atilt. "What's up?"

Travis looked past Mia at nothing particular. "I won't be going on tour with Mr. M after all. Seems he had to cancel for some personal reason."

Mia leaned toward him. "But you got a sub at the theater. You'll be out a month's paycheck and –"

Travis put up his hand to stop her. "Mr. M handed me a check for my month's wages when he told me. He was very insistent I take it."

Mia sat staring at him.

"That's not all," Travis said. "When I stopped in at Johnny's to see Blake he said he'd overheard that Mr. M's tour money was going toward buying a bookshop."

"What? Why a bookshop?"

"Don't know. Maybe it was a good investment or something." Travis grimaced. "I could tell Mr. M was trying to hide how upset he was."

𝄞

Blake and Jaz, feeling bad for not keeping up with R.G., stopped in to see him on their way to play at Johnny's. Blake hated that he wasn't better at caring for the old musician – after all that he tried to do for them.

Finally, after a minute of knocking and calling out, R.G. opened up and shuffled back with the door.

"Hey, kids…good to see ya."

"Just wanted to check in. Know you're not feeling all that great," Blake said.

"Come in 'n have a seat. We need ta talk."

Mike's grand piano called out to Blake but he fought the urge to play and sat across from R.G. and Jaz at Mike's chrome and Formica table. After a moment R.G. lifted his head and spoke in their direction.

"Couple things. I'm movin in with Mike and his family this weekend. Lord…I've never met such kind folks. Guess they're worried about me. And it does get lonely here."

Jaz moaned. "Sorry –"

"Jaz, no need to say anything." R.G. held up his hands. "You're doin' what you should be doin'. It's fine."

Blake wanted to add something but decided against it and sat back studying his hands.

"'Nother thing. Mike is pretty disappointed he can't buy that bookshop." R.G. paused.

"Why a bookshop?" Jaz questioned.

R.G. chuckled. "He got this idea of turning it into a coffeehouse. Not because it's been his dream to go into business but rather to have a place for musicians starting up – like you."

They both knew the only reason they had a job was because of the agreement between Mr. M and Rudy.

Jaz scowled, pinched her lips and peered at Blake. "We need to help Mr. M."

Blake hunched his shoulders and looked at R.G. "Any idea's how we could do that?"

R.G. was silent a moment then grinned and leaned back. "Yeah, a couple. Think you can get your gang over here?"

𝄞

With help from Travis making calls and meeting up with Abby and Cobi at the Y café, back from their deadend trip west, the apartment was filled with angst, hormones, and resentment. But *La Familia* was together once again – scattered around on the sofa, piano bench, and the floor.

R.G. wasn't quite sure where to start but first needed to get something off his chest.

"To begin with…I want ta apologize for not helpin' you kids better when Mr. M. was gone."

Abby groaned. She stood up from the floor, walked up to R.G. and hugged him. "We're all here now because of you."

Blake popped up and joined Abby, putting his hand on R.G.'s shoulder.

The rest immediately swarmed in with hugs and pats on the back.

"You're an inspiration to us just being you," Blake said.

Jaz reached for his hand with a pained expression. "I need to finish what I wanted to say earlier. Thank you for taking me in. I wasn't in a very good place..." Jaz leaned in and kissed R.G. on the cheek.

R.G. cleared his throat. "All you kids got such talent. Let's figure a way to use it ta help Mr. M."

𝄞

The next three hours seemed to vanish in an instant. With R. G. serving as catalyst, drawing on his thirty years of playing for a living, a creative and daring plan was hatched to raise some cash for Mike's café idea. They would break up in teams of two to four and play in public spaces all around the city: subway platforms; outside Grand Central Station; the ferry terminal to Staten Island; LaGuardia airport – to snag folks waiting for cabs; on the steps of the Metropolitan and Guggenheim Museums; and, of course, Times Square in the evening for the ones that weren't already working nights. However, the thing that really grabbed everyone's imagination was Travis's idea of performing in costume. Each person was to develop a character or persona that would draw more attention to them, adding a bit of theater to their performances while providing anonymity for the shyer ones.

Working together on a plan that would help their beloved Mr. M seemed to alleviate the tension of broken relationships, misunderstandings and guilt. Once again they had a common goal. They even coined a name for their spontaneous performances, Whiz Gigs – not knowing how long they'd be allowed to play at some of the locations before they would have to whiz off.

When R.G. sensed it was time to wrap up, he made his way to the piano, sat down and played a few measures to get their attention. Everyone stopped talking and turned to see who was playing.

"What? Didn't know you could play!" shouted Cobi.

R.G. finished up and held the last chord with his head tipped back. "Hey...no big deal. Anyone can play this thing," he laughed. Then in a whisper, "Yeah, okay. That's all I got."

With that they all rushed him, laying it on thick how he could be the next Stevie Wonder or even Ray Charles, which R.G. ate up with both hands.

After take out pizza from Gino's and more good natured jivin' and blather, the impromptu meeting came to a close as a couple of them needed to get to evening jobs. They agreed to meet back with R.G. in a couple days with ideas about music, costumes and ways to "encourage" people to give up their cash for their music.

Seeing the last of the kids out the door, R.G. scuffled back to the piano and sat down. *Thank you, Lord, for these kids.* It has been a long time since he felt so needed.

Mike sat at the breakfast table peering silently at his mother. He hadn't felt such pain since hearing his father had died of a stroke. After Noah left his lap, gasping with sobs, it became clear what he had to do – cancel the tour, even if it meant damaging his career. He called all the musicians to explain the situation and all were very understanding – not so, however, when it came to his agent, Jimmy. Once again he had let down an important resource in keeping his career alive. But when Noah had fallen asleep in Mike's arms, after he told him he wasn't going anywhere, he knew he'd made the right decision.

Mike leaned on the table, puzzled by his mother who studied him with a sweet smile.

"What? You know my career is all but over," he said a bit snarkier than he meant to.

His mother continued smiling – which bugged him.

"My dear son. You've made one of the most important decisions you'll ever make. And I'm so proud of you."

Mike simply shook his head, got up and ambled to the piano in the living room. While he sat rummaging through his brief career as a musician and composer he slowly worked himself into a frenzy, pounding out his pain with an extemporaneous purge – driving his hands up and down the keyboard – moaning as he attempted to hold back tears. After minutes rocking back and forth with frenetic catharsis, he finished with a gasp, held his head and slumped over the keys.

His mother walked in, sat next to him and reached around him for a hug. "Michael, don't despair. I have something for you to consider."

$\oint$

R.G. was first to be called the next morning with the good news. Mike was moving forward with the apartment and bookshop. Explaining his farsighted father once again came through with money he had set aside not only for his children's education but also twenty-five thousand when each reached a responsible age. And his mother determined that time was now. But he told R.G. not to say anything to the kids until the deal was complete – knowing much could still go wrong. The only one knowing what both Mike and the kids were up to, R.G. was beside himself with joy. Overnight it seemed he had gained a surge of energy and was beginning to think he might beat vile ol' Mr. C – if he kept feeling this good. His head was filled with ideas of what the kids could do to raise money. Thanksgiving was coming up next week, then Christmas after that.

$\oint$

With R.G. moving in with the Monroe family over the weekend, Friday afternoon would be the last chance to gather and firm up plans for the *Whiz Gigs*.

R.G. was nearly scared out of his wits when a thunderous crash then a thud and some moaning came from his door.

He hesitantly opened up to Carlos lying on his back with Tobias trying to help him up – both arriving on roller skates.

"Hey, R.G.," Tobias said as he retrieved Carlos' beat up guitar from the floor.

"What in the world, boys? Tryin' ta give me a heart attack with all that racket?"

"Sorry," muttered Carlos. "Still gettin' the hang of these skates. Thought they would add a unique twist to our roving minstrel outfits."

R.G. cringed at the word minstrel, fearing what their costumes might look like.

Abby and Cobi arrived before Carlos could get upright, swooping up the stairs with capes, (actually beach towels) flowing from their shoulders.

"Well…can you guess who we're going to be?" both standing erect with arms crossed over their chests.

"Mr. and Mrs. Clean?" cracked Tobias.

"What a hurtful thing to say. We're Wonder Woman and Superman. Don't you see the capes?" Abby said, trying to maintain a stern expression.

While they argued over what would be a proper pose for a super hero, Mia and Travis arrived in the elevator with bags of take-out Chinese food.

Turning to the clunk that announced their arrival, there was much puzzlement, squinting and laugher along with attempts at guessing their characters.

"Think Disney," Mia shouted over the guffaws while Travis stood silent behind her appearing like he wished he were somewhere else.

"All right, all right. So our costumes need a little more work," Mia said after no one came close to guessing right. "Ever hear of Cinderella and Prince Charming?" Mia asked, appearing frustrated.

"Ah…actually that was on the tip on my tongue," Cobi said, then burst out laughing so hard he fell back down – rolling onto his side.

"All you gangstas better get in here before I get kicked out and have to vacate early," R.G. said, standing at the door, chuckling to himself.

Eager to get on with eating, plates quickly filled of moo goo gai pan, kung pao chicken and fried rice with chop sticks clicking.

Halfway into their feast there came a strange mixture of atonal cords and jangling coming from the hall. Everyone turned to the door as if a magnet had pulled their faces.

"Wow…wonder who this could be?" Cobi sniped as he headed for the door. But before he got there it swung open and Jaz paraded in jingling a tambourine and wearing an alluring golden robe, Egyptian headdress and leather sandals – laces crisscrossing up to her knee. She stopped and stood as if accessing which one of them would be allowed to kiss her ring, which she held out to the assembled masses.

"Oh man, if it isn't Cleopatra. And let's see…is it Caesar or Marc Antony with the accordion?"

Although R.G. couldn't see all the outfits that paraded into the apartment, he hung his head.

𝄞

Before the kids left the meeting, R.G. had talked them into more appropriate costuming. This wasn't Halloween after all. With much heated debate, R.G. led them into accepting a Charles Dickens Victorian England theme for outfits. Which in turn would lead to trips to thrift shops and Goodwill stores for: wool overcoats; vests; top hats; cloaks; newsboy caps; long skirts; scarves; shawls; waistcoats; and bonnets.

After shopping all the next day the only items they couldn't find or make do by alteration were bonnets and top hats so Abby decided to make her own – Mia and Jaz going with hooded cloaks. And Travis would borrow a couple top hats from the Winter Garden Theatre prop shop where he was working. After R.G. moved in with Mike, the kids agreed to meet next time at Abby's Grandmother Nana's apartment on the Upper West Side to put it all together and lay out a performance schedule.

𝄞

"What am I doing?" Mike groaned, Saturday morning – first light peeking into their bedroom. "I hate the idea of running a business. Why am I …?"

Naomi reached over and lightly touched his lips with her fingers. "Shh…" She then rolled on her side and turned his face to hers. "You have people who care about you who can help."

"I loathe keeping records, my check book never balances and –"

Once again Naomi's fingers quieted his lips. "Stop it. You don't have to figure it out by yourself. Why don't you check in with Rudy today after you help R.G. move in?"

"I almost forgot." Mike heaved a sigh. "I need to go to the doctor with him this week. There must be something that'll help him."

𝄞

The Monroe family station wagon had plenty of room for R.G. and his meager belongings. Before heading down with the last of R.G.'s things, Mike stopped at the door and looked back into the vacated apartment – his beloved grand piano with the scarred lid appeared abandoned.

R.G. sensed Mike's pain. "Sorry, Mike."

Mike couldn't speak right away and paused to collect himself.

"How do you move on when something so wonderful has passed? All the memories – sweet, bitter, highs, lows. Seems I spent a lifetime in that room."

R.G. reached and found Mike's shoulder. "We have many lives – chapters that we are given to live out. You're heading into another one that will be as meaningful. Just different."

"I don't know what I'm doing with this bookshop business, R.G. It scares me."

"Trust, Mike. Did you always know how things would turn out while you lived here?"

Mike had to chuckle at that. "Hardly ever," he said. It felt good to laugh.

27

Plans

Mike would deal with moving his piano after he knew where in the world he would land next. But he had the flat for another eight months, having paid a year in advance so R.G. would have a decent place to stay. He was sure some kid could use a place to crash at times or he would maybe sublet to a musician.

After leaving the apartment behind, with all of R.G.'s belongings in the car, it felt good to stop in and see Rudy – something familiar.

"Well, well..."Rudy said, in an exaggerated snarky tone, seeing Mike and R.G. at the end of the bar. "You guys here lookin' for work?"

Mike wanted to go around the bar and give the old buzzard a hug but figured he'd get smacked before he had a chance.

"Rudy...I need some serious consultation. Looks like I'm going ahead with the bookshop café. But I'm keeping it from the kids until I have it for sure."

Rudy looked off around the bar like he was conjuring up some great insight. "Sure, I can let you in on my trove of business knowledge. But it'll cost ya."

Mike had an idea where this was headed. "Hope it don't cost much...don't have much."

"You got enough. How about you and R.G. play a couple of numbers and I'll pass along everything I know."

Mike turned to R.G. "What do you think? I could get your horn from the car."

"Man, let's do this," R.G. said with a huge grin.

After setting R.G. up next to the piano, Mike reached for the microphone and addressed the customers that were on their way home from work, scattered around at tables and at the bar. He recognized most of them as regulars.

"I would like to introduce you to one of the most talented, humble musicians I've ever known...Reggie Green, known as R.G. to his many friends in the business." Mike put his hand on R.G.'s shoulder. "Think we'll just mess around for a while and see what turns up."

R.G. nodded in agreement.

A few of the customers acknowledged R.G. and stood, applauding loudly. R.G. grinned.

For almost an hour piano and sax intertwined with inspired melodies and rhythms that transported the growing crowd on a once in a lifetime journey. Mike dug down deep to unearth feelings that lay buried beneath the drama of the last three months. A tribute to his son emerged first bringing some tears but then R.G. picked up the thread and brightened the emotions with lyrical wisps of joy – causing Mike to smile in spite of himself. R.G. then took the lead and presented a medley, paying homage to great musicians past and present – Mike picked out a Ray Charles strand and hammed it up swaying side to side as he played. With the bar filling to capacity, everyone in the room – whether standing or sitting – had turned toward the minuscule stage. It seemed the early customers had called friends to hustle over to Johnny's.

When Mike sensed R.G. was running on empty, he slowed the pace and ended the impromptu concert with *People get Ready* – R.G. playing sweet counter melody over the top of Mike, causing some in the audience to sway side to side – eyes closed as if dreaming.

The roar of applause and shouts of *encore, encore* were deafening at the end of their final number.

Saturday being the busiest night of the week, the scheduled evening entertainment arrived at seven just as the ovation was dying down – Jaz and Blake stood at the entrance with mouths hanging open. When Mike saw them, he motioned with his head for them to come over.

"Just warming them up for you guys," Mike said and hugged his protégés after they wove through the crowd to the piano.

𝄞

After a trip to the bookshop and apartment on Monday, Mike and Rudy sat at a donut joint across the street to hash over possible scenarios.

"Well?" Mike asked, cringing slightly, waiting for some reaction from Rudy.

Rudy turned his head and gazed out the window over at the forlorn little shop across the street and pursed his lips in thought.

"How bad do you want to do this?" he said, looking back at Mike.

"Crap, Rudy. That doesn't sound very positive."

Rudy rubbed his forehead. "Sorry, Mike. Just that there's a lot to consider. First off, you don't have much for a down payment but I guess they're willing to work with what you have. Trouble is your monthly payments end up a little high. And, of course, the money down is gone if you can't make payments. But…if it goes good for a couple of years they might consider lease to buy for another 5 years."

Mike groaned and slumped. "That seems like an eternity right now."

"You'll need some cash reserve for slow times, an accountant and reliable help, people that won't skim from the till. If you plan on serving food, there'll be regulations to follow and periodic inspections. Then there's utilities to keep up with and security issues." Rudy stopped and leaned back in the booth. "You do have one thing going for you though. The Mob probably will leave you alone. You won't be making enough for them to bother with."

"So there is a silver lining in all this?" Mike snorted and hung his head. "I don't think I can do this."

Rudy called the waitress over for more coffee then continued. "Mike, I know you pretty well. The only way this is going to work is if you hire a good honest manager. You and Naomi aren't cut out for the business side. But I suppose it's possible to make it work if you can keep good talent coming in. That and offer something unique."

"What might that be?"

Rudy puffed out his cheeks. "I don't know. That's for *you* to figure out."

28

Secrets

Naomi was getting concerned Sunday morning after calling for Noah with no response. She went up to his bedroom – empty. She hadn't heard him leave the house but headed for the back yard to check. Before she yelled his name, she saw his huddled form in the back corner of the small yard under the ancient apple tree he loved to climb. Just able to hear his murmuring she watched as he played with small sticks and rocks covered with scraps of fabric. Naomi sat down on the back steps to watch him playact. As best she could tell it was a scene where he was leading a band of friends from danger to a safe tree house he made from chunks of wood he had found behind the shed. She became alarmed when Noah started shouting for the rocks and sticks to hurry before they would be captured. But when they had reached the safety of the tree house he quieted and started singing. The singsong rhythm of the verses touched her heart.

"Have a no fear…I a here."

"No ting…get ya now."

"We a safe…we a strong."

"Stay to getta…all day a long."

Naomi hated to disrupt this intense tableau but it was time for a quick breakfast and then church. She called to him, then headed over and gazed down at her precious child.

"What are you playing, dear?"

Noah looked up at her with the steely countenance of a military general.

"My friends need my help to keep 'em safe."

Naomi thought back to their time in Liberia and never saw Noah with another child – ever. She wanted to ask more questions but they needed to get going.

Rose called from the backdoor for them to hurry if they wanted to eat. As Naomi gathered up her son and carried him into the house, she had an uneasy feeling about Noah's play. *Something happened to him in Africa.*

$$\oint$$

Mike and R.G. were already at the table when Noah came in. Mike immediately grabbed his son and pulled him onto his lap.

"Mike, that child needs to sit in his own chair. He's a big boy now," Naomi said, as Rose raised her eyebrows at them.

"I just need him for a minute. I've missed him so."

Noah wiggled off his lap with a coy smile like he was looking for his father to grab him back onto his lap. He wasn't disappointed – Mike snatched him up but then ran around the table with Noah screeching wildly.

Rose leaned over to Naomi and muttered, "I think his father, Lewis, just showed up." She said it with sad eyes, but also a slight smile.

"Okay," Mike said, plopping Noah in a chair next to him. "I haven't heard any plans 'bout Thanksgiving yet. It's Thursday isn't it?"

His mother looked at him like she expected there was something behind his question. "Okay. What's on your mind, Michael?"

"Well…because it's a family day I was hoping to invite the Y kids over to tell them about the café idea and see their reactions. I want to make sure this makes sense to them."

Rose squished her face. "You know I love those kids to pieces but isn't it a little late to invite them. Won't they have plans with their own families?"

"I was thinking any time they can drop in or maybe get most of them here later in the day after time with their families. And, as you know, most of them don't have a lot going on at home." Mike sauntered up to his mother with a syrupy grin and gave her a squeeze.

"My good husband lives on. Seems you've picked up all the tricks of getting your way."

Mike looked around to her face as he held her, appearing hopeful. "So…is that a yes?"

Rose rolled her eyes, gazed over at her grandson and back at Mike. "Of course, Lewis."

Mike knew he had her, knowing this could be the last Thanksgiving dinner in their home.

$$\oint$$

R.G. didn't like lying to Mike and Naomi about where he was going after church but felt he'd be forgiven – telling everyone he was meeting an old friend he hadn't seen in years.

Rose gave R.G. a surreptitious little chuckle as he was heading out the door and said, "Have a lovely time with your friend."

He snorted and stopped briefly. *Can't get anything past that woman*, he thought, casting a boyish smirk her way.

He was thankful he could now afford an occasional taxi to get around – with the generosity of the Monroe family.

R.G. half expected some comment from the cabby, but got none (a little disappointing), after he told him the address of the Majestic Apartments on Central Park West – one of several homes of Abby's grandmother, Nana.

When the cab pulled up to the imposing twin towers of the apartment complex overlooking Central Park, the kids were already hanging around out front waiting for him, to the chagrin of the doorman.

All but one of *La Familia* swarmed R.G. as he stepped from the cab like he was a visiting dignitary. He was thankful to Nana for opening up her place to this rowdy bunch and knew he could trust her to assure the costumes and music were appropriate. In short, he needed a woman's perspective.

He was not disappointed.

29
Thanksgiving

R.G. knew better than to try to keep a secret from Rose. So after he got back from his meeting with the Y kids, he found her alone in the kitchen planning for what could be sixteen guests for Thanksgiving.

R.G. stood in the doorway to the kitchen and tapped his cane so as not to startle Rose who was working on something at the table with her back to him.

She jerked around and smiled. "Ah…there you are. How's your *friend* doing?"

"Rose," R.G., said, bobbing his head, "the CIA has nothing on you."

She laughed. "It comes with having kids. So…guess you're here to come clean."

Rose got up and ushered R.G. to a chair across from her and sat facing him.

"Yes, but it's 'pose ta be a surprise for Mike," he said, laying his cane in his lap. "The kids got wind that Mike's tryin' to buy a bookshop and turn it into a coffeehouse but may not have 'nough to pull it off. So they decided to raise money by goin' around playin' on the streets durin' the holidays.

When they tole me their plans, I didn't have the heart to tell 'em dey wouldn't make much. I know this…havin' played on the streets myself."

Rose reached for his hand. "You did right by encouraging them. Mike will be touched."

R.G. was quiet a moment, then said, "Love can cause you to do crazy things."

"I expect you understand that pretty well."

R.G. gave Rose a crooked little smile along with a nod.

Rose sat studying R.G. "How are you feeling these days? You're looking good."

"I think it's workin' with those kids. They can drive me nuts then practically bring me ta tears wid kindness. Don't think I could ever be a parent though."

"You are parenting if you realize it or not. You must know they love you but most don't know how to express it."

R.G. sucked in a breath like he was taking in nourishment. "Thank you, Rose…for helpin' me wid the kids and havin' me here. It means the world."

"Your very welcome, my friend," Rose said, and squeezed his hand.

𝄞

Trina arrived late the evening before Thanksgiving with a surprise friend (a boy) from Mississippi who didn't have time, or money, to head home for the holiday. Only getting three hours notice, Rose was put on the spot – Trina calling as they were heading out from Cornell. What could she say at that point but 'of course'.

The house was filling up fast! Noah gave up his bedroom to R.G. and moved to a floor mattress in Mike and Naomi's room in the downstairs bedroom. Trina would bunk in with her mother, and Persis and Jesse were already asleep in Trina's old bedroom when she arrived. The boy "friend" got the last remaining spot, a pull out couch bed on the back porch. Although, not getting to bed herself until well after midnight, Rose was in seventh heaven.

Getting everyone up and out the door by nine AM was a logistical maneuver only slightly less daunting than the D-Day invasion.

The weather still holding at fifty-two degrees and sunny, Rose led the march the four blocks to Harlem Baptist church – where Reverend Robinson (James) was waiting on the front steps, a grateful glimmer radiating from him upon seeing Rose leading her clan.

$\oint$

Mike sat at the end of the pew feeling all this had happened before. Then it hit him. That night two years ago at the Plymouth Theater – his family spread out next to him to celebrate the premiere performance of his musical *The Girl in the Yellow Scarf*. Sweet. A silent prayer of thanksgiving flowed from him.

The Reverend seemed especially on fire as he reminded the congregation that thanksgiving should be a daily practice and, yes, thanking God for everything, even for the challenges in life, lest we become self-centered, allowing pride to seep in. This was something Mike knew he had to work on – daily.

Mike knew the Reverend was from Detroit so was looking forward to baiting him into a bet on the football game today – Giants vs. the Lions. Although the Lions were doing better, Mike wouldn't give up on his Giants. With the game on at one, he had some negotiating to do – mainly with Mother.

By now the family knew the drill. Mother was the captain and the rest of the family were the grunts. She was determined to have everyone served by one o'clock, despite Mike's pitiful attempt at negotiating an earlier time because of the game. Not knowing exactly how many Y kids would show or at what time, Mother wisely had a buffet style meal – he knew went against her deep-seated formal upbringing. But this left the possibility of wandering into the living room to catch a glimpse of the game – the volume turned down real low.

Mike knew something was up though when he answered the door to Mia and Travis with their instruments and dressed in Victorian era costume.

"Okay." Mike said. "What's going on, you two?"

"A surprise," Mia simpered. "You'll find out later."

Not appearing a bit surprised, Mother rushed into the dining room with greetings and hugs. *Huh.*

The grunts, having done their duty to Mother's terse commands, stood around the table for prayer then dug into the feast spread out before them. After Mike filled his plate, he positioned himself at the end of the dining room table so he could catch a glimpse of the kickoff, about to happen any minute, on the living room TV. Unfortunately, the Reverend positioned himself at the other end of the table pretty much blocking Mike's view with his rather imposing stature. He could easily have been a Giants linebacker himself.

After everyone was at the table, except Cobi, Mike had to find out what was up.

"Okay. All right. I guess I'll need to ask what's going on because no one is volunteering any information."

All the kids looked around innocently until Blake finally spoke up. "R.G. can explain. It's all his idea."

"Hey! That's not true," said R.G.

"Well?" Mike asked.

"Your kids…" R.G. started.

"My kids?" Mike jumped in, grinning, looking down at his son.

"Yes, they're your kids. After hearin' 'bout you wantin' ta buy a bookshop and turnin' it into a coffeehouse, *they* had this idea ta help out by playin' for money on the street. I must say they done better than I ever done."

Mike brought his hand to his face and peered around the table at each one. Blake stood, walked around the table and handed Mike an envelope stuffed with cash.

30
The Opus Café

"**W**ell, with the kids invested guess there's no backing out now." Mike said, staring out the downstairs bedroom window at the night. Naomi was tucked in close and Noah was asleep on the floor mattress beside their bed.

"Mike, I knew you were going to do the café when you first mentioned it."

"What...you been taking lessons in mind reading from my mother?"

"Chalk it up to intuition. That and I finally think I've got you figured out."

Mike turned to her. "What do you mean?"

"You will do just about anything for those kids, including going into business – which we both know is not your strength."

Mike bowed his head and moaned. "How're we going to pull this off? I got the distinct feeling Persis has no interest in getting involved."

"She stepped in once to save you. Perhaps she is waiting to see how serious you are about this."

"I can't involve her anyway. She's overloaded with the stores and then there's becoming a mother soon."

Noah stirred from his mattress and they both lifted up to peer over at him. After he rolled over and continued sleeping, they lay back down and faced each other.

"I'm sorry. I'm so used to charging ahead to handle things by myself. I don't want us to move ahead with this if you aren't a hundred percent for it. We're equal partners now."

"Mike, if I didn't agree, you would have known it by now. I think the café is a good idea. You were there for me in Liberia. You can not *imagine* what that meant to me."

Mike pulled Naomi in close and she wrapped her arms around him. "So what do you think we should do with the money the kids gave us?"

Naomi thought a minute. "It should be something tangible that they can see. Not cleaning equipment or anything practical like that."

Mike rolled a couple thoughts around in his head. "Something I thought of when I first walked up to the entrance. I pictured a sign in the front window – The Opus Café. They would see that every time they came in. It couldn't cost more than the $234 dollars they raised."

"I like that because it includes them." Naomi snickered, "However, we do get to live upstairs."

Naomi had a way of covering him in a blanket of peace. He was so thankful he gave in to his heart and followed her. If he hadn't, he could have lost her – forever.

$$\text{𝄞}$$

Rose was in her glory as she took breakfast orders from each of her family and guest as they sauntered into the kitchen Friday morning. This is what she lived for. The first to show up was Noah in his pajamas who slammed into her from behind with a hug and a giggle. Rose put down her spatula, scooped up the precious child and gave him a hug and kiss then, cradling him, walked to the downstairs bedroom and knocked on the door.

"Morning, kids."

"Morning, Mother," came a sleepy reply from within.

"I've got Noah. So no need to rush this morning."

There was a thump on the floor then shuffling to the door. "Oh...you're the best grandma ever," came Mike's hushed voice from behind the door – then a click to lock it.

Rose turned with a knowing smile. "I know," she murmured on the way back to the kitchen with her treasured grandchild's head nestling in her neck.

About an hour later, almost everyone had found their way to the breakfast table – served by Rose and her helper Noah. Conversation was infectious and warm: R.G. and Jesse replaying the action in the Giants win yesterday; and Persis happily listening to Trina and her friend complain about the cafeteria food then laughing at the pranks they pulled on their hall mates. Finally, everyone sitting around with their second cup of coffee, Mike and Naomi wandered in all smiles. Jesse squinted over at his wife then lifted his chin to address the latecomers.

"So...glad you two could make it. Trouble waking up?"

"Wow. Someone's a little green this morning," Mike said, fighting a smirk.

"Green?" Noah piped up from across the table. He looked around at the various shades of skin – dark to light – then studied Jesse. "He's not green, Papa."

Mike erupted with a spasm of laugher, practically falling off his chair.

Jesse appeared like he was trying mightily to control himself and said, "See there, Mike, out of the mouth of babes... wisdom. You could learn a thing or two from this bright child."

Mike eventually controlled himself and explained the expression to Noah who looked like he sort of got it, then asked his father if he could go play in his room. Mike nodded, but then motioned for Noah to come to him. When he came within reach, Mike snatched Noah onto his lap. "Where have you been all my life, son?"

Noah appeared puzzled and said, "Waiting for you, Papa."

Mike pulled him in for a hug and fought back a sniffle – tears coming to others around the table.

The morning spent at breakfast wove yet another strand into the fabric of the Monroe clan – something Mike felt as he took in the various conversations. It was good to be home. Now, on to making The Opus Café happen, and by the way, try to make a living at it.

$$\text{\clef treble}$$

Heading to Chelsea to sign papers for the bookshop, and bundled up for the first snowfall of the season, Mike and Naomi stood in four inches of slush in front of his Mother's waiting for a cab.

Jumping in the back seat of the taxi, a swirl of snow following them in, Mike settled in and reached for Naomi. "I don't think I would have the guts to do this without you."

Naomi smiled. "I know you've been stressing, so that's why I thought getting the kids involved with the layout would be fun. So when we're done at the realtors, they're planning to meet us at the bookshop. Thought it would remind you why you're doing this."

Mike's anxiety ebbed with the thought of the kids. When they pulled up front of the little shop, he knew he had made the right decision. Everyone but Cobi was there with broad smiles, greeting them like royalty. One of them had made a

2'x2' cardboard sign and taped it to the front window – The Opus Café printed in an arc then under it, in a reverse arc in smaller letters, Music and Food.

𝄞

Mike felt like he held the key to Fort Knox as he opened the door of the little shop. The kids swarmed around him anxious to get a look inside. Mike barely got the key out of the lock when they rushed past him like escaped puppies to explore all the nooks and crannies around the room. The bookshop had once been a bar, then a coffee shop, then a restaurant and had remnants from each business. Just inside the door, was an L-shaped counter with stools. The other walls had floor-to-ceiling bookshelves with a slightly raised platform at the end of the room on the right, apparently once a small stage. Tobias and Carlos stepped onto the platform and looked out as if, by the looks on their faces, imagining something wonderful. Mia and Travis tried out the stools at the bar and Blake and Abby wandered the shelves checking some of the books that were left behind. Jaz pretty much shadowed Mike and Naomi like something was on her mind.

"Well, what do ya think, Jaz?" Mike asked, motioning to a small café table with wicker chairs.

Jaz looked out over the room then peered at Mike from the corner of her eye. "I'm not exactly a business person but… how do you expect to make any money selling coffee to a bunch of teenagers?"

"Hmm." Mike paused and rubbed his chin. "Guess we need to do more than sell coffee. Think we should get everyone together to brainstorm ideas."

Jaz looked doubtful as Mike shouted for everyone to pull up chairs and stools for a meeting. He leaned back in his chair and gazed around at the eyes fixed on him.

"Jaz just asked me how the café is going to make money. I have some thoughts but I would like to hear any suggestions you might have – and remember, there are no bad ideas because any idea can morph into something we can use."

Mike began writing down suggestions reminding them to think outside the box – offering something original could help bring in new customers. After some typical suggestions were thrown around, eventually some creative ideas came up.

1-Food: A specialty pizza, soups, sandwiches, fresh baked bread, a special sauce for spaghetti, chili, and subs – all fairly simple to make but each with the Opus twist. Carlos said the opus twist made him think of some kind of pastry. Mike liked the idea and said he'd run it past the bakery across the street to see if they might come up with something unique. Involving other businesses in the area would be a win-win and would help get the word out. Mike knew he could count on his sister Persis with ideas for preparation and suppliers after they decided what they wanted.

2-Drinks: Tobias seemed interested in experimenting with adding different flavors to existing soda claiming he never drank just straight soda, adding a slice of fruit or splash of ginger or even some kind of spice. He said he would make up a taste test for next time they met.

The kids were really getting into brainstorming but were in need of some fuel to continue. Naomi already had it planned. She arranged for Eddie's Pizza, down a block, to deliver food and drinks – which arrived just as the energy level was beginning to ebb. They all seemed pleased with themselves as they exchanged ever-increasing crazy ideas – some not so bad.

Finally, with pizza boxes empty, Mike got their attention and brought up the next item for discussion.

"From the sound of it, we're going to eat pretty good. Hopefully we can sell some to the customers. But I think what we really want to do is to be able to play, experiment, entertain, learn, share and maybe even teach."

"Teach?" Jaz and Tobias shouted in unison.

Mike let the idea simmer a moment. "Yeah, teach. I'm not talking Julliard level, but you could easily teach beginners. I know a couple of you first learned from a neighbor or someone in your family. It's just a thought, but I think some of you might find it rewarding."

"Okay, okay," Jaz said, "are we going to get a chance to play or are we just going to sling food and teach a bunch of brats to play chopsticks?"

"Jaz...you have such a way with words. Yes, you will have a little time once in awhile to play."

"Wait...once in awhile?" shrieked Jaz.

"Sorry...just kidding," Mike said with a crooked smile. "Now, thoughts on entertainment? And know that none of this will be set in stone and can morph as time goes on."

Ideas where batted about like beach balls along with shouts, laughter and some indignation. But they ended up with some doable ideas.

The performing hours could feature different genres to reach a broad range of people. There could be an open mic time to encourage and give experience to new performers. Performers would have to commit to a schedule a week ahead. The space in the back used for shipping/receiving for the bookshop could be turned into two soundproofed practice rooms and made available for sign up.

Naomi said she would type up the notes for their next meeting. Mike said he would have his sister, Trina, who was thinking of becoming a designer; draw up a preliminary layout for the space. And, with Rudy's help, he had gotten permits and inspections expedited along with reliable carpenters and painters. All in all, he was hoping to have a grand opening on New Years Eve – three weeks away. He knew this was a little crazy but thought it was doable. Now all he had to do was find a dependable manager. This was probably the most important part of the whole deal.

After the kids headed out he sat alone with Naomi wondering if he had really messed up big time. How in the world could he find a trustworthy person who loved kids, was tolerant and smart, that he could work with? Then it hit him. But he would have some major selling to do.

Mike and Naomi were buttoning up their coats and about to head out when Cobi pushed open the front door and slunk in.

"Sorry I'm late."

Mike stood with Naomi studying the latecomer and noticed a distinct dark ring around one of Cobi's eye.

"Wow!" Mike exclaimed. "What's with the eye? Looks like that might have hurt."

Cobi looked away. "Got mugged in Madison Park."

Mike knew there was more to the story but let it go for now and summed up what they had talked about earlier but Cobi was reticent, which was unlike him. Going on dinnertime, Mike wanted to understand what was really going on so with a nod from Naomi invited Cobi to dinner with them.

31
Crunch Time

Once again Mike found himself in a tight spot. *What was I thinking?* Only a couple weeks until the grand opening. Not just the café but get moved in to the apartment that would save their commute time from Harlem. At least the painting was done upstairs so the furniture they ordered from Macy's and that his mother gave them could be moved in.

"Sorry you married me yet?" Mike asked Naomi as they headed out the next morning for Chelsea, leaving Noah with Grandma.

Naomi gave a sarcastic chuckle. "Not yet...but getting close," she said, then let out a little snort.

"What?"

"That's just your MO. Its part of why I love you...I suppose," she said, hugging his arm in the back of the taxi.

Mike was buoyant thinking of the great time they had with the Y kids yesterday, but then thought about their drummer. "Think Cobi is going to be okay? I don't like that he's at war with his father. My dad never hit me although I gave him cause at times."

Naomi thought a moment. "With his mother out of the picture I think there must be added stress between them. I like that he leveled with us and knows we're here for him. He does need to show his dad respect though. He took off for California with Abby without saying a word until he called from LA."

Immediately, Mike thought of when he dropped out of NYU before saying anything to his father causing a fissure that never got restored before his father's death. He would keep checking and help Cobi understand the importance of reconciliation.

"I noticed how he responded to you. Think you're a mom to most of the Y kids."

"I'll do everything I can. I know how it feels to lose a parent."

Mike shook his head and snickered. "Remember thinking I wanted us to have a lot of kids some day. Just didn't think it would happen so soon."

$$\oint$$

Knowing Mike was in over his head, Persis met him at the bookshop to help, even though her due date was looming. With Naomi off volunteering at Noah's school, she had Mike all to herself. She set up a simple accounting system that even her math deficient brother could follow – lined him up with food suppliers, a list of regulations to follow, inspectors and an insurance agent. She then organized a small office in the back with a Rolodex with all the contacts he would need. All this she accomplished in about three hours time and only cost Mike an order of Chinese carryout for lunch.

"Pers…what can I say…you've saved me again," Mike uttered with a sheepish grin as they sat at the counter of the café.

"Sorry, I should have volunteered sooner, but I wasn't sure how serious you were. Call any time if you have a question. But I do recommend you get a manager ASAP."

"Actually Mia managed her family's restaurant for awhile. She seems to have a gift in accounting along with the cello. That and she wants desperately to move out from her parents apartment and live on her own. This job along with playing in a theater orchestra would help her do that."

"I know she had a thing for you."

Mike puffed. "I think she has her sites on Travis now. We'll see what happens."

After catching up on the news about Jesse's latest novel and sister Trina's life at college, Persis waddled out with Mike to the curb to catch a cab.

Mike leaned over her belly to give her a hug and kiss. "Sorry for being a rotten brother and leaving you stranded with Father's stores. I just couldn't deal with them back then."

"Mike...I found I enjoy managing and I'm really good at it. It all worked out."

Just as the cab pulled up to take Persis to Harlem, one of the painters ran out. Mike's mother had called. He needed to get home immediately.

Mike told the painter to tell Naomi where they'd gone when she got back with Noah – then jumped in the taxi with Persis.

32
Life and Death

When R.G. moved to Harlem, Jaz started making regular visits to see him before heading to her evening gig with Blake at Johnny's. It finally sunk in that the legendary sax player wasn't going to be around forever. Their discussions usually centered on music and ranged from breathing techniques, proper embouchure and dynamics to debating the merits of renowned sax players. They would argue at length about style – ranging from the smoky gentleness of Ben Webster to the jazzy funk of Grover Washington to the breakneck speed of Charlie Parker's bebop. But, mostly, R.G. wanted to encourage Jaz, assuring her if she kept at it she could become one of the best.

As Rose waited for Persis and Mike to get back from their meeting at the café, Jaz showed up at the door to check in on R.G.

Appearing worried, Rose ushered her in. "I don't like how R.G. seemed this morning so I got an appointment for him later today. But, go on up. He's so looking forward to seeing you."

Jaz immediately headed upstairs. Getting to his bedroom, she peered around the half opened door. R.G. appeared to be sleeping so she turned and was about to head back down when R.G. stirred.

"That you, Jaz?" he whispered.

"Hey. I'll come back later. You should get your rest," she said from the door.

R.G. coughed. "Got eternity ta rest. Come on in."

Jaz felt anxious – he didn't look so good. She pulled up a chair to be close to him. It seemed he labored to speak.

R.G. turned to her. "How's Johnny's goin?

"Rudy doesn't like any Avant-grade, bebop or free jazz. So it's getting kinda boring."

R.G. let out a slight snort. "Folks don't go ta Johnny's ta be challenged musically. So stick with the standards but play best ya can. You'll get the major clubs someday."

Jaz nodded. "You seem tired. How you doin'?"

"Not ta worry, I'm gonna be fine." R.G. paused. "You try them Rico reeds yet?"

"Yeah, you're right. They're great."

"Good."

Jaz waited as R.G. shifted to lie on his side. He held out his hand to her. She took it in hers.

"You gotta know this whole family loves you – me included," he said.

Jaz looked away and started to pull her hand back but he held on. "Please, stay."

Jaz dropped her head.

"To receive love you have ta believe you're worthy," R.G. said softly. "Think you're worthy?"

Jaz kept her eyes downcast. "Don't know."

R.G. sighed. "Let me tell you then. You are precious and you are worthy. I love you like a daughter, Jaz."

She gasped...then whimpered. "Love you, too."

Jaz wasn't sure what to do and peered over at the door. She fought the urge to leave – but gave in and leaned over the bed and crumpled into R.G.'s outstretched arms and wept.

R.G. waited for her weeping to stop then spoke low in her ear. "I wanta give you somethin' that's precious ta me…'cause you're worthy." Jaz slowly sat up, wiping her eyes.

"Actually, two things," R.G. said, nodding toward the sax case sitting on the desk. "First, my mother's Bible that's always with me in that case. After I went blind it meant even more. I could hear her reading to me as I turned those dog-eared pages." R.G. paused to draw in a long slow breath. "Next thing in there is my King Super 20 sax. Lot of the greats love that ax…and so do I."

Jaz sat back. "No, no. I can't."

"Jaz, please." R.G. lifted his head. "It means everything to know you'll be cared for – mind, body and soul."

Jaz reached over and stroked his sunken cheek. "*You* are one of the greats…R.G."

R.G. smiled and slowly laid his head back on the pillow and closed his eyes.

Jaz grasped his hand and watched as his breathing slowed… his chest rising…then falling…rising…then falling.

𝄞

After Rose talked to Mike on the phone, she tried to busy herself in the kitchen getting a snack ready for when Noah got home from school. She had called Jesse, who was working from home, to come to dinner – intuiting the family needed to gather in support of R.G. When Persis and Mike arrived, they immediately went upstairs. Quietly stepping into the bedroom, they found Jaz sitting beside R.G. clinging to his hand.

Looking up from the motionless old musician, Jaz searched for something to say but could only bow her head and sob.

♭

Even though doctors informed the Monroe family nothing could have been done for R.G., Mike sank into despair leading up to the funeral. He had lost not only a prized member of his band but a father figure as well.

Searching for some inspiration as he sat at the living room piano the night before the funeral, Noah came down from his bedroom for a good night hug and kiss. Coming up to Mike from behind, Noah stopped and studied him.

"What's wrong, Papa?"

Mike hadn't heard him approach. He turned to Noah and shuddered briefly, "Oh…there you are." Slowly his melancholy ebbed as Noah came up and hugged Mike around the waist. Mike was struck by the timing of his treasured son. He was in the midst of trying to let go of R.G. when Noah appeared – exuding grace.

"I miss R.G., too," Noah said.

"Thank you," Mike said, into the air as he pulled Noah onto his lap and smothered him with an embrace.

♭

Harlem Baptist Church was packed to the rafters. Every folding chair that could be found filled what open space there was in the narthex, aisles and balcony – folks standing shoulder to shoulder along every wall.

Mike was able to contact members of his old band *The Gathering* to play at the funeral and, with much cajoling, Mike convinced Jaz to take R.G.'s place on sax, connecting her with the top musicians in New York. Reverend Robinson insisted the group play up front, spread out behind the pulpit, with Mike directing from the piano.

This would not be a solemn affair but a celebration and tribute to a beautiful soul. The service started with the band playing *When The Saints Go Marching In* and ended with *Amazing Grace*, with Jaz featured on the sax.

$$\text{\clef treble}$$

The week after the funeral was a hectic time of moving into the apartment for Mike and Naomi – Mike also playing the role of construction supervisor to get the Café ready for the grand opening on New Years Eve while getting rehearsal time in with *La Familia*. Naomi stayed busy setting up the apartment, helping with the Christmas program at Noah's school and shopping with Persis to get ready for her baby. And Noah seemed to be adjusting to his new school, PS 11, that was only a block and a half away. Either Mike or Naomi would walk with him but after two weeks he was getting teased about being a baby and needing his parents to walk him. So far, he didn't care. He liked their time together. Often, after school, Noah would go up to the third floor attic where he had an elaborate setup of empty cardboard boxes to play with his action figures. But, weather permitting; he would play behind the apartment in the small patch of yard.

After a quick stop at his mother's to pick up mail (especially royalty checks that hadn't been forwarded), Mike ran up a flight of stairs to their new apartment in Chelsea with two takeout bags of soul food from his favorite restaurant in Harlem. He was determined to enact a regular dinnertime that his mother always insisted on – not easy with the chaos of moving and Christmas only two days away.

Walking into the small kitchen with a big grin he caught Naomi at the stove about to start dinner.

"Surprise!" Mike shouted as he set the food on the kitchen counter. "Got some down-home cookin' in these here bags."

Naomi turned from the stove and, seeing the food, sighed with relief. "Oh…bless you. I've been running all day to get things done."

"Figured you'd be busy. Where's Noah?"

"He's been out back since getting home from school. Not sure what he's up to but I haven't seen him for over an hour."

Mike moved the bags of food to the table in the kitchen then was hanging up his coat in the hall by the door when Noah came up the stairs behind him.

"Hi, Papa," Noah said with his arms wrapped around a small shaggy bundle of black fur.

Mike smiled at first. Then fighting a grimace asked, "What'd ya got there?"

"Isn't he a beauty?" Noah asked, lifting the creature's matted head so Mike could see its face.

Mike hesitated a beat. "He's something alright."

Just then Naomi came out from the kitchen with dishes to set the table, stopped mid-stride and made a face with a curled lip.

"I wondered what that smell was," she said, not able to take her eyes off the mutt. "Noah, he stinks." Setting the dishes on the table she covered her nose with her hand. "Take him outside."

Noah's face fell. He looked down at the little beast. "But he needs me."

"Son, you don't know where he's been," Mike said. "He could have rabies for all you know."

Noah slumped down cross-legged on the floor and snuggled the scrawny mongrel then peered up at his parents. "You dint know much 'bout me."

Naomi turned away to hide a snicker. But catching Mike's expression, sadness swept her face.

Mike rubbed his forehead. "Maybe he belongs to someone, Noah."

"But…maybe not," Noah countered.

Mike looked at Naomi for help.

"I don't know," she said. "But both of you reek to high heaven so, before we do anything, into the shower. Then we'll discuss what to do."

Noah's face sprang from utter despair to a glowing beam of hope. Mike and Naomi looked at each other and moaned in unison.

While Noah and the dog were in the bathroom, Mike peered sad faced at Naomi and advocated for his son – saying he always wanted a dog but pets weren't allowed because Persis had allergies. Naomi turned from Mike, muttering. But after ambling to the window and back she relented – on one condition. They would post notices around the neighborhood with a description in hopes of finding an owner. Mike knew, however, with no collar or tags the stray was probably Noah's, but the dog would need a trip to the vet.

When the stink had been washed down the drain, boy and mutt came out of the bathroom – mutt wrapped in a towel in the arms of Noah in his underwear.

"He smells good now, Mama."

33
Christmas Child

Finally, after weeks of racket from renovating the downstairs, Mike stood in silence scanning the bookshop turned café. He couldn't help himself. He went out to the street and looked in the window as if seeing everything for the first time – like a new customer. The earth tones of wood flooring and molding, along with muted amber walls with teal paneling made the interior appear cozy and inviting. Looking in the window from the street, the coffee bar beckoned with gleaming bean grinders and a huge commercial espresso machine. Heading through the glass-paneled door, the layout was open – the bar and stools on the left, a dozen small round tables with café chairs scattered in front of a slightly raised stage in the back right hand corner. Inexpensive poster art hung everywhere with indirect blue, yellow and red spot lights splashing the walls and stage. He could hardly believe this was his – but not just his, really.

Mike had about five minutes of peace until Noah and Naomi burst in from the street with armfuls of packages. They were trailed by a cab driver with more packages.

"I know you hate shopping but you could at least help," Naomi said, catching Mike gazing over from his seat at the bar.

"I just now sat down," he pleaded.

"Okay," Naomi said, "but I do hope you like wrapping presents."

"I'll do anything you ask, just not shopping," Mike said, going to grab the packages from the taxi driver and giving him a tip.

Noah had dropped his parcels on a table and ran to the little office in the back corner behind the bar where his dog would stay when not upstairs or out back on a lead.

Coming out with the broadest grin possible, Noah walked up to them – the furry runt in his arms licking Noah's face. "Think he missed me."

Peering at Naomi, Mike lit up as well. "See the joy in that boy's face?"

"Uh, huh," Naomi said. "I'm just thankful it got shots from the vet."

"One thing though, Noah," Mike said. "The pooch does need a better name than doggie."

Noah hunched. "What do you think, Papa?"

"Well," Mike reached for the mutt from Noah and lifted him up to study him. "He sure is skinny and curly."

"Skinny's not a nice name, Papa," Noah said frowning. "But I like Curly okay."

Naomi's mouth twitched slightly – but turned into a smile. "Cute name, Noah." Then with an aside to Mike, "Maybe we could find two more strays and name them Larry and Mo."

Mike let out a little snort and whispered, "Now you're talking trash, girl."

♪

With the arrival of Christmas Eve, most *La Familia* members were busy with their families. Blake, hoping to keep confrontation at home to a minimum, talked Abby into coming with him to dinner at his parents. He in return agreed to spend time with Abby and her grandma, Nana, after presents were opened Christmas day – Abby's parents deciding to remain in Europe over the holidays. Mia had invited Travis to her family's traditional Christmas Eve dinner and celebration. Cobi, Tobias and Carlos were sequestered by their families but itched to be out partying with friends.

Rose, along with having all her children and grandchild home for a couple of days, made sure Jaz and her mother, Iris, were welcome for Christmas day dinner. However, all plans were suddenly altered after the Christmas Eve service at Harlem Baptist. While everyone was having a nightcap of hot cider and mulled wine in the living room, Persis let out a shrill shout from the upstairs bathroom.

"Jesse!"

The scene in the living room could have been one from a Norman Rockwell painting. A nine-foot spruce was heavily laden with tinsel and ornaments accumulated from over twenty-five years – many handmade "treasures" from elementary school projects of the Monroe children. The fireplace gave a soul-quenching glow from the end of the room. The adults were in quiet conversation or gazing at Noah fighting to keep his eyes open, sprawled on the floor with his canine pals, Curly and Jesse's yellow lab, Charlie.

Upon hearing his sister, Mike poked Jesse sitting next to him. "What'd you do now?"

"How could I do anything wrong from here?" he replied with a scowl.

Mike was about to list his possible infractions when a second more blood-curdling scream rang out.

Suddenly the meaning for the cry registered and everyone turned wide-eyed to Jesse.

"Guess I better..."Jesse said, leaping up, stumbling at first to get to the stairs.

𝄞

No one wanted to be left out. After Jesse, in near panic, drove Persis to Harlem Hospital on 137th Street the rest of the clan arrived, taking up most of the waiting room chairs. But, at a little past midnight, when it appeared the actual birth wouldn't be for another ten to twelve hours, the excitement waned and all but Jesse returned home – Noah remaining asleep the whole time in Mike's arms.

At 11:36 the next morning, Jesse was nudged awake as he slumped in his waiting room chair.

"Mr. Peterson, you can see your wife and daughter now."

𝄞

Once again the Monroe Strivers Row home was in a state of chaos. Trina and a roommate were home for a week from college. With the hospital just two blocks away, Jesse moved into the downstairs back bedroom to work nights on his sequel manuscript due last month while visiting Persis and the baby during the day. Rose insisted on having Noah for the week leading up to the Café opening, claiming it would free Mike to focus on rehearsals with *La Familia* and working with Mia, his new store manager.

After finishing up the Sunday dinner dishes, Rose had corralled her rascally grandchild for a bath when Jaz showed up at the door.

"Come in, dear," Rose said – one hand on the doorknob and the other arm holding onto a giggling retired street urchin – Curly barking his approval of bath time for Noah.

"Let me guess. Bath time?" Jaz said, coming in with R.G.'s sax.

"I wanted to get the job done before you got here but we got sidetracked playing a game of hide-n-seek."

After R.G. passed, Rose encouraged Jaz to continue her daily visits before going to her evening gig at Johnny's. It seemed Noah and Jaz had developed a bond that Rose felt was good for them both.

"I suppose we can put off tub time for awhile," Rose said, and let Noah loose so he could plow into Jaz for a hug.

Jaz looked at Rose with a huge grin, Noah wrapped around her waist. "I think we can finish our little composition by the opening. This boy is quite a storyteller."

"Tell me about it. He comes up with something new every time he hears the tub water running."

Jaz laughed, grabbed Noah's hand and they headed up to the fourth floor studio where they would work on their surprise composition based on Noah's backyard play. Jaz was completely blown away by the child's imagination. When Noah first performed his play for her, it touched her deeply and she immediately thought of composing music to go with the story. She'd never considered anything like this before. But if she had learned anything from Mr. M it was to listen to her heart. And she allowed herself to do just that when it came to Noah.

$$\text{\textphoninenote}$$

With all the distractions of the holidays, Mike and Naomi had their hands full rounding up the Y kids and getting them to focus. After a brief celebration with family over the birth of the baby, named Rose Marie (Mother overjoyed by their choice), Mike and Naomi returned for a peaceful evening in the Chelsea apartment above the bookshop before an all out press over the next six days to get ready for the grand opening of The Opus Café.

Mike knew the Café would be a financial challenge by not serving alcohol. But, with the help of his "board of directors" as he jokingly called them, he felt they had something unique. Rudy from Johnny's had concocted a dozen non-alcoholic drinks using a variety of tropical juices, tonic water, grenadine and fancy glassware. Al, the manager from the soup kitchen, had put together a simple but tasty menu that could be easily assembled in their small kitchen: specialty soups and chili; individual pizzas; and hot sandwiches. The bakery across the street had fun dreaming up a line of desserts that appeared exotic but were simply made from sheet cake, whipped cream and a drizzled topping of fudge, caramel or butterscotch. His sister, Trina, designed a logo and a single page menu that would vary for each day of the week. Al also helped lay out the small kitchen for efficiency: a four-burner stove; pizza oven; a large Panini grill for sandwiches; a large double-door fridge; and a commercial dishwasher.

Mike slipped downstairs early after a cuddle with Naomi to sit quietly with his coffee and pour over his notes. He needed waiters, cooks and a maintenance crew. Fortunately, between Persis and his old friend Al, he had interviews this week to hopefully get who he needed. He had also offered jobs to the Y kids in hopes of keeping some of them out of trouble. Lastly, he had to get the remainder of his things from his flat in the Village that he was cheaply sub-letting to Travis. And, now that Travis was working during the day and performing at night, his kid-brother Robbie, who he was taking care of, agreed to stay with an aunt and uncle in Brooklyn for the rest of the school year.

Satisfied that he had things under control *for now*, Mike moved to the piano on the stage and as *La Familia* began to arrive he played *We Are Family*. As each of the kids burst in the door they ran to him, laughing, to get their instruments and join in. When Jaz and Blake finally arrived, Blake stood clapping to the beat and Jaz couldn't help but grin, dancing in to get out her sax. Standing next to Travis on trumpet they both played, swaying to the beat. Jaz's radiant joy warmed Mike's heart, negating some doubts he was having about the Café. To bring *We Are Family* to an end, Mike got up from the piano to let Blake take over and danced and sang his way to the front of his band of misfits.

"Wow! Are we back or what?" Mike hollered bringing the song to an end.

Not wanting to quit, Cobi and Tobias slid into *Celebration* with drums and guitar. Abby and Mike grabbed microphones and bopped around the stage singing for all their worth to an imaginary crowd of thousands.

Grinning ear-to-ear, Mike tried several times to end the song but nobody was having it. Then Naomi was drawn from upstairs into the revelry and it went on for another twenty minutes with: *I Wish*, *Car Wash*, *Love Train*, and finally *Ain't No Sunshine*.

When Mike finally brought the impromptu concert to a close, *La Familia* seemed to have regained the cohesion they had shared at Radio City. They actually were smiling at each other – all of them.

34

The Opening

Mike couldn't ask for a more picturesque evening. Fluttering confetti-like snow falling amid yellow taxis trundling along on 8th Avenue – smiling folks in scarves, mittens and winter coats, scurrying out front to get to New Year's parties. At times the city appeared anew. This was such an evening.

Mia came up behind Mike and inquired softly, "Mr. M. Think we're ready?"

He turned and suddenly became aware of the clatter and shouts of his Y kids doing last minute preparations. Carlos, Tobias and Cobi had taken the role of house-band for now so were adjusting equipment and warming up on stage. Mia, acting as café manager, was holding a meeting to go over the jobs for the evening. Along with performing, Abby, Travis, Blake and Jaz would also help in the kitchen or serve tables. All in all it seemed a miracle. Mike had each of the Y kids tethered in some capacity to the functioning of the café.

"Well, do *you* think we're ready?" Mike asked grinning at the nineteen-year-old who was probably more capable than he in running the place – but he wasn't about to tell her, at least not for a while.

Mia scanned the hubbub and shrugged. "Sure. We got this."

Mike let out a chuckle knowing there were endless issues that could arise with this crew.

Mike was curious what traction his small ad in *Variety* would have, hoping his name might still be a draw. Along with the kids plastering posters everywhere possible, he prayed they wouldn't get skunked. To his amazement, however, it wasn't long until the Café was packed to capacity with a crowd peering in through the front window.

Mike stayed out of the way to see how much the Y kids could handle. All bases were supposedly covered with Mia's schedule of who was where and when: kitchen, serving and playing.

Naomi came in from upstairs with Noah tagging behind, his head swiveling to take in the crowded room. She sat down next to Mike and leaned over to catch his attention.

"Well?"

Mike turned as if woken from a dream. "We'll see. The playlist covers a dozen genres, but the kids insisted on it." Mike rolled his eyes. "But there is something for *everyone*."

"Jaz said they've planned a couple surprises."

"Oh?" Mike said, pulling Noah up onto his lap.

Blake, acting as MC, hopped onto the small stage and reached for the microphone, exuding a confidence that surprised Mike.

"Happy New Year everyone and welcome to the grand opening of The Opus Café. This is the brainchild of Mike and Naomi Monroe. Maybe you've heard of them."

A roar of applause and shouts went up as the crowd turned to them. Mike snorted but grinned from his station at the end of the coffee bar.

Blake continued. "I think it only appropriate though that Mr. M start us off with the first song. Not one of his compositions though…but a blues number"

Mike wrinkled his forehead and peered at Blake through his eyebrows.

"We recently discovered that he is a closet harmonica player. Something he should be proud of. Also, we know his favorite blues man is Taj Mahal."

Mike feigned a scowl at Naomi with a tight smirk. "Traitor!"

"So we're ready to backup Mr. M in his all time favorite… *Walkin' Blues*.

Mike handed Noah off to Naomi and grudgingly stood with his palms out. "Sorry, I don't have my harp with me."

Blake roared. "Oh…no problem. We found one in the piano bench…where you keep it hidden."

Mike shook his head. What could he do but head to the stage – Noah clapping wildly.

When Mike reached the platform, he whispered in Blake's ear. "I own you, man. Maybe we should wrestle some time." Mike was collegiate champ in his weight class at Cornell.

Blake responded. "Wouldn't be fair. I've got twenty pounds on you."

"Good one." Mike guffawed at the lanky teen.

Mike heaved a sigh, buried his harp in both hands and wailed a two bar intro as Carlos on guitar and Cobi on drums jumped in along with the others, settling into the classic 12 bar progression. It wasn't long before Mike was all in, jammin' to the smokin' hot standard. Mike couldn't believe it. Guitar, sax, bass, and drums, okay, but blues violin, cello, and trombone? Somehow it worked. *These kids can pull off anything.*

The crowd loved it – going nuts when the impromptu blues band finished along with the Y kids laughing themselves silly at Mike, feigning humiliation.

Mike tried to look stern, shook his finger at each of the kids and mouthed 'you're going to pay for this' as he escaped the stage, not wanting this evening to be about him.

Blake immediately grabbed the mic. "Let's hear it for Mr. M…Mike Monroe."

Mike lowered his head and made his way back to his seat at the end of the bar.

Noah reached out to him. "Oh, Papa! Teach me to do that."

"What? To make a fool of yourself?" Mike said with a snort catching Naomi's sweet gaze.

"I mean play the harmonica."

"Sure, as long as you keep up your piano lessons."

Noah bobbed his head enthusiastically.

Mike hugged his dear child. "It's bedtime, my son."

Noah got a look of horror and looked toward the stage waving his arms like he wanted to be rescued.

Naomi reached for Mike's arm. "There's another surprise for you."

Jaz suddenly appeared holding out her arms to Noah. "I need to borrow your boy for a while."

Mike looked to Naomi – puzzled.

"They've been working on an opus of their own in the upstairs studio," she said, hunching her shoulders.

"Are you sure you want to do this now?" Mike asked.

"You need to see this."

"Okay," Mike said with a crooked smile.

Noah skipped away with Jaz as the house lights dimmed – a yellow spot lighting the center of the stage.

Reaching the platform Noah sat down with his head bowed in the circle of yellow light – his back to the audience. Mike held his breath, bringing his hands to his face.

A simple piano intro portrayed a lifting sunrise with Noah miming a child waking from a dream. He stood looking around with his arms outstretched. Suddenly he stopped as if seeing someone and reached out to imaginary friends, inviting them to come sit with him. From the darkened background, Abby began a narrative that followed Noah miming to an imaginary band of innocents sitting in front of him. Other instruments of *La Familia* joined in to follow the story with melody and harmony.

Mike could hardly believe it. He unconsciously reached for Naomi's hand and turned to her.

She whispered, "The kids have been working on it all week in your old flat in the Village."

For the next five minutes, Noah pantomimed a struggle with an evil being in the rainforest of Monrovia, *La Familia* enhancing the depiction with dramatic music. Mike was a little unsettled by the ferocity of the portrayal, wondering how his son would have experienced such conflict. He made a mental note to ask Naomi what she thought. Happily the frightful drama of mime and music gradually evolved into what seemed an eventual rescue and redemption. It all seemed too heavy for an almost seven-year-old giggly boy.

As Noah's heartrending story came to a close, *La Familia* stepped out from the shadows and formed a half circle behind Noah. Travis set his horn aside, scooped up the boy and set him on his shoulders. Noah thrust out his arms like he was about to take off flying and chortled as the band left the stage weaving between the tables single file – playing a victorious song, half rock-n-roll, half march. With the crowd nearing hysteria, the parade stopped in front of Mike and Naomi to bring the triumphant opus to a close.

Putting their arms around each other Mike and Naomi grinned helplessly at the band of teens topped with a glowing African boy from the rainforest of Liberia.

After high fives and hugs from all the kids, they returned to the stage and Naomi headed upstairs to put Noah to bed. For Mike the evening couldn't get any better but he wondered what other possible surprises they had up their sleeves. He didn't have to wait long before seeing Liz Shepard walk up to him as the band started up, Tobias setting the beat to *Play That Funky Music*, with Cobi singing lead and the others rockin' back and forth with their instruments.

She stood there with a coy smile. "Mike Monroe…a business man?" she said over the loud funk rock.

Mike pursed his lips and slid off the stool. "Time will tell," he said into her ear.

He reached for a hug and offered his seat. "You look radiant. Glad you could see this." Then it hit him. "Oh, I get it!"

"Yeah, Blake called. Thought it might be fun to do a couple numbers from Persis' wedding."

"Smart kid. Having a Broadway star show up couldn't hurt business."

Blake's face practically split from a grin, seeing Liz next to Mike at the end of *Wild Cherry*'s song.

Mike squinted at Blake – flummoxed. "Can you believe this kid? Mr. Mellow has turned into Soul Train's Don Cornelius."

Liz reached for Mike's hand and squeezed it. He peered at her, wondering what was going on…hoping Naomi would come back soon.

"Folks, we are in for a rare treat." Blake reached out his arm to where Liz was sitting. "I see Liz Shepard, the star of stage and screen, has blessed us by stopping by."

Always the diva, Liz burst into a grin. She rose from her seat like a budding flower and swooped to the stage, brushing Mike's cheek with a kiss on the way.

Mike didn't like what he was feeling. *What is she doing?*

When Liz got to the stage, she spoke into Blake's ear and motioned for Abby to join her at the mic. After a brief intro from Blake at the piano and Cobi on drums, *La Familia* roared off into *Dancing Queen*, their favorite from Persis' wedding. The only trouble was people could hardly contain themselves. Many of the girls leaped up and boogied between the tables knocking over drinks.

Mike hoped Liz would slow things down before tables got tipped over. She wisely did that at the end of the song – giving Abby a warm hug, the crowd reaching a greater roar than ever.

Liz waited for the crowd to settle then mouthed, *All You Need Is Love*, to the band. Grins broke out as they slid into the iconic Beatles' song.

Mike sat back, drenched in a flood of emotions as scenes from the past couple years scrolled in his mind: playing at the Central Park band shell with Sarah only to lose her hours later; sitting backstage in a wheelchair as he watched *La Familia* mesmerize the audience at the Radio City Music Hall; playing a battered upright piano amidst the scattered remains of a schoolroom with the love of his life at his side – their son appearing to them from out of the dense rainforest of Liberia. Seemed all the significant events in his life revolved around music.

"What is it, love?" Naomi said, coming up to him after getting Noah to bed.

Mike blinked. "Oh, ah…just drifted off a bit."

"Go have some fun. I think the kids would like to do another song with you."

Mike looked to the stage as Blake was playing, *Yesterday* – singing the Beatles song with a passion that surprised Mike.

When the song ended Mike peered at Naomi. "I believe the kid has already passed me up."

"Impossible. You're one of a kind." Naomi nodded to the stage. "Go ahead now, and show your stuff."

Thankful for Naomi's bright smile, Mike headed for the stage. Blake got up from the piano and bowed to him. The room went silent as if waiting for something grand. Mike looked back at his wife and threw her a kiss then addressed the audience.

"I would like to dedicate this Stevie Wonder song to my wife, Naomi, because...*You Are The Sunshine Of My Life.*" Audible ahhh's rose up around the room. Mike gazed across the crowded Café and sang to her as if no one else was in the room. Naomi held his gaze the entire time, radiating joy. Feeling the love in the room, he slid into another song: *Forever Young* with Liz and Abby jumping in to sing backup. Each time he came to the lyrics 'may you stay forever young' he swept the crowd, pointing to each table as he beamed.

Closing in on midnight, Mike needed to let the kids take over so immediately stood up with the last chord of the Bob Dylan classic and motioned for Blake to take over. Blake seemed reluctant amidst the standing ovation – Mike deflecting the thunderous applause holding his hands out to his young protégés.

Looking out into the grinning faces of the young crowd, Mike caught sight of Leon Kohn giving him thumbs up. The producer of his Broadway hit *The Girl in the Yellow Scarf* gestured for Mike to come over. Mike was thrilled at first, thinking about reconnecting with Leon, but then got a sudden shiver. He saw someone that looked like Marcus, the contentious Liberian, walk away from the front window. *Is that possible?*

35

A New Year

Mike gazed out at the street past the CLOSED sign on the Café door – yellow cabs still driving about delivering late night revelers. After checking if everything in the kitchen was turned off and in order, Mike wearily headed upstairs.

"Where have you been?" Naomi asked, propped up in bed watching him get undressed.

"Sorry. Checking things out downstairs," he said, slipping in next to her.

"It couldn't have gone better, don't you think?" Naomi said, cuddling into her favorite position at his side.

"All in all pretty good. Got a chance to reconnect with Leon Kohn. However, from my perch at the bar I observed some dealing going on out front. I need to check in with Cobi to see what that was about. And it seemed Jaz had words with a couple hoods until Travis stepped in and convinced them they should leave. He can appear pretty intimidating. I think I'll add bouncer to his job description. Then there was a really upset girl that cornered Carlos. Tobias stormed off after seeing them going at it. But at least Mia was kept busy playing manager and Abby and Blake could be reigniting their flame."

"Boy… you don't miss much do you?"

"Comes with being a wrestler. Always watching for trouble."

"Thanks for the warning."

"What trouble could you give me?"

"Not tellin'. But you better watch it…" Naomi yawned deeply and rolled onto her side.

Mike thought briefly about some lovin' but let it go as the image of Marcus reappeared. But he didn't see any reason to upset Naomi by bringing it up. He might just be visiting. But why wouldn't he come in to see them?

𝄞

There were few traditions Mike held fast to but watching the Rose Bowl game New Year's Day was one he never missed. And he needed to watch it in his mother's living room in Harlem with a bowl of taco chips, salsa and a root beer (not needing to nurse a hangover with a Budweiser this time). He and his father would always make a buck bet, Mike always getting to choose first. But in all the years, his dad had won eight out of ten. Mike was eager to continue the tradition with the Reverend, hoping to end his losing streak.

After a little time with Jesse, Persis and the new baby, Mike watched the pregame commentaries with Noah at his side – strategizing on how to engage the Reverend in a bet when he showed up.

Jesse walked into the living room cradling Rose Marie so Persis could get a nap. "Are babies allowed in here?"

"Depends," Mike said. "Who's she rooting for?"

"The winner."

"Who might that be?"

"UCLA, of course. Michigan doesn't know how to play in warm weather."

"It's tempting to bet her but it wouldn't be right taking money from a baby."

When the game was over, Naomi came downstairs to get Noah ready for bed – deciding to spend the night in Harlem and head home after church tomorrow. Walking up to Mike she could tell it hadn't gone well for him – seeing his disgruntled look at the Reverend's outstretched hand.

"I'll put your money toward a new basketball for the youth," Reverend Robinson said with a chuckle.

"I see you kept your losing streak alive, dear," Naomi snorted.

"Don't want to talk 'bout it."

Changing the subject, the Reverend asked how the Café opening had gone.

Mike was happy to move on from the game. "Reverend, I couldn't be more proud of those kids. Got more applause than I ever did at Johnny's."

Persis nudged Mike. "Don't forget to ask him about your idea."

"Yeah, I was going to get to that." Mike looked beseechingly at the Reverend. "Persis had this idea." Hearing that, Persis shook her head in denial.

"All right, we had this idea. Seeing how well the kids did, we think they would go for a fundraiser for the orphanage to help replace what was lost in the storm."

The Reverend took about two seconds in thought. "I like it. As you know, we can get about two hundred and fifty into the fellowship hall. I think folks would be generous especially after meeting that beautiful boy of yours."

Mike hesitated. "Ah…"

"Yes? Something else?" Reverend Robinson asked.

"Think we could do it for three evenings; Friday, Saturday and Sunday? Would be great if we could raise as much as possible."

"I don't think that's a problem. Most folks heard the kids at you sister's wedding and I think they could spread the word to fill three nights."

Mike couldn't ask for more. Not only could they raise money for a good cause but also the kids were happiest when working together on a common goal.

After saying goodnight to everyone, Mike and Naomi headed for the back bedroom with Noah already upstairs in Mike's old room.

After they crawled into bed, Naomi sat up and peered down at Mike. "What's going on? I thought you'd be excited about the kids performing again."

In spite of giving the kids a new challenge, Mike couldn't help a creeping melancholy. "I am. Just thinking of all the years in this great old house. Not easy letting it go."

Naomi reached over and gave his cheek a little pinch. "So…would you rather stay here with your *mommy* or come live with me and your son?"

Mike didn't appreciate her little joke at first. "My mommy?" But then catching her coquettish grin his sadness vanished and he reached for her – thankful.

36
The Plan

Once again Mike was flying high and couldn't wait to contact the kids with the fundraiser idea for the orphanage. He wanted to get them together as soon as possible to get their buy-in and come up with a theme for the performances. With work and school for some, the best time to meet was noon on Saturdays.

Mike had three large pizzas delivered to the Café ready for their arrival. He then sat at the coffee bar to catch a glimpse as they came up the sidewalk. He had to chuckle to himself, realizing how much working with these misfits meant to *him*.

As they came in, each one walked up for a handshake or a hug but he didn't explain anything. He just motioned to help themselves to the pizza and sit at the tables he pulled together in front of him. The munching of pizza seemed to add to the anticipation he was hoping to create. He sat silently smiling until all had arrived.

"Ladies and gentlemen." He stood and addressed them as if an assembly at the United Nations, "We are gathered today for a noble purpose."

All heads turned from their pizza – eyes widened.

"As you know, Noah came to us from an orphanage in Africa. We were sent to help start a school in a temporary building until a permanent school could be built." He thought a moment how to phrase the next part. "But, after funding for the new school dried up and a storm wiped out the old structure, the much needed school was put on hold."

Puzzled looks began to appear.

"So…what would you think about performing a fundraiser to help rebuild the school?"

Slowly the idea of playing again as a group seemed to catch their imagination.

"When would it be and what music would we play?" asked Jaz.

"Depending on how much original stuff you wanted to try, I figure about four-to-six weekends of practice once we've got a play list worked out."

Some smiles began to spread.

"Of course, we can try out music on the customers here at the Café. I know Mia has all of you scheduled to play off and on throughout the week."

Blake held up his hand. "You mentioned original *stuff*."

"Yes. Now that you've played our own composition for Radio City, I'm hoping we might do more. As a matter of fact I would challenge each of you to come up with some ideas. I don't care how crazy. Anything goes at this point."

As Mike let the challenge marinate, Noah bound in from the upstairs apartment with Naomi trailing behind. Streaking across the room he crashed into Mike for a hug.

"Papa!" he shouted bending back to look up at him. "Guess what Mama bought me today?"

"A new toothbrush? A pair of socks?"

Noah scrunched his face looking pained. "That's boring, Papa."

"Sorry. I'll try to be serious. Tell me more."

"You make music with it."

A stab of guilt shot through Mike. With all that was going on with moving and setting up the Café, Mike had neglected giving Noah his piano lessons.

"Give me a hint."

Noah held up his hands spread out about a foot. "It's this big."

The kids couldn't help themselves and started guessing.

"A piccolo, tambourine, a drum…"

Noah turned around to face them shaking his head. "No. No. No. It's a recorder."

Mike winched at the word *recorder* – remembering the painful squeaks and squawks from prep school. It was probably his least favorite instrument. He looked past the kids to catch Naomi's eye. "What?"

"We were passing a music store and he wanted to go in," she said. "The salesman at the store suggested it and showed him how to play a scale. When Noah tried, it was as if he knew just what to do. You need to hear this."

"Can't wait," Mike said with a forced grin.

"Really, Papa? I'll go get it," Noah said, running off – all excited.

"Oh boy," Mike muttered.

"Okay," Mike addressed the kids again. "While we wait for Noah, you all have any thoughts about doing this fundraiser?"

The kids looked back and forth between themselves. Then Travis stood. "Could you give us a minute?"

Mike hunched his shoulders. "Sure."

Travis nodded to the back of the Café and the others followed him there.

As the kids huddled in the back, Noah ran in with his shiny new instrument, holding it out to Mike.

He took it and examined it as if he'd never seen one before. "Wow! This is so cool, Noah."

"Want me to play something, Papa?"

Mike's eyes grew wide. "Sure son. Maybe later," he said, seeing the kids coming back.

Noah's face dropped. "Later?"

"Oh…" Mike said feeling Naomi's glare.

As the kids were sitting down Mike smiled at his son. "Hey, troupe. Seems Noah has something to play for us. What do you think?"

The kids were all in, turning their chairs so they could face him – nodding and smiling.

Noah didn't hesitate and moved in front of them and started playing. Mike wasn't prepared for what he heard. This was not a sound from grade school. The kibitzing between the kids immediately stopped. Naomi held her hand to her heart while Mike squinted, trying to fathom what he was hearing. The image that came to mind was a haunting call or beckoning of some sort – a request to gather with some urgency. But gradually the breathy quality of the instrument changed to a calming repose. At the end of his brief concert, Noah stood as if he had vanished, unaware of were he was.

Naomi knelt down in front of him. Mike peered over her shoulder to get a sense of what his son was feeling. "Noah, that was wonderful. What…" Mike wasn't sure how to ask him where the music came from. "Where did you learn to play that?"

"I don't know, Papa. Just playing it for my friends."

After Noah's extraordinary solo, the kids told Mike they would play for the fundraiser – on one condition; Noah would be part of it. Mike had already thought of weaving Noah into the playlist. But he let on that it was their idea.

37

Life is what happens...

Chelsea

"I know your plans are all about preparing for the fundraiser but don't forget, we're meeting with Noah's teacher right after school," Naomi reminded Mike as he was heading out of their apartment.

"Oh, yeah." Mike turned back from the open door. "So, are we going to hear *again* how he isn't fitting in? He daydreams all day. He doesn't contribute in class. His reading needs to improve. He –"

"Enough, Mike," Naomi cautioned. "I promise if it's the same old story…I will homeschool him. I didn't get an education degree for nothing."

Mike closed the door and went to sit facing Naomi at the kitchen table.

"I like the sound of that. But…" Mike paused to formulate his proposal.

"I know," Naomi said. "He needs to be around kids his own age. Someone other than Curly."

"Not only that, I think we need to consider some arts training. You saw how natural he was performing at the Café party."

Naomi moaned. "That was both amazing and a little frightening. Why couldn't he be good at math or science or anything other than…acting?"

Mike chuckled and reached for her hands. "'Fraid he's a natural, sweetie."

Naomi leaned back with a sigh. "Lord help us. Another artist."

$\oint$

Gramercy Park

"So. This is it?" Jaz groaned as she peered over at Blake, both at a darkened corner table at Johnny's.

"What did you expect? Least you're doing what you're good at."

"Think Rudy should give us more nights. Three just isn't cutting it," Jaz snarled.

"You know he's committed to the quartet for another six months. Maybe when they move on we can pick up another night or two."

Jaz shook her head. "It's not just that. We're stuck, man."

"I know. I'm beginning to wonder if I should have gone to med school, like I planned."

"Don't start that. Trust me. You'd be miserable – wondering what it would be like playing for a living."

Blake couldn't help but snort. "Out of the mouths of babes."

Jaz pulled back. "Watch who you are calling a babe, preppy."

Blake heaved a derisive sigh.

"Sorry," Jaz said. "Know you don't like being called that." Changing the subject she added "How are you and Abby these days?"

"She's different. It's pretty much over since her little trip to LA."

"Oh…" Jaz said and gave Blake a peculiar look that sent a chill through him…or was it a thrill.

Brooklyn

A cab screeched to a halt within inches of Carlos' knees when he started across Flatbush Avenue. His mind mired with thoughts of Sophia practically got him killed. *Great, getting run over would solve everything.* With the cabby still leaning on his horn, Carlos mouthed 'I'm sorry' and hustled back to the curb.

Surviving the next two blocks to Tobias' grandma's duplex, Carlos stood on her porch and knocked, wishing he were anywhere else. Grandma Brown peered out the front window with the curtain pulled back.

"Carlos. Come on in," she said stepping back from the door. "What's with the long face, child?"

"Ah…just looking for Tobias."

"He's workin' at the grocery store up on Brooklyn Avenue."

"Oh. Yeah. I'll stop and see him there."

Grandma Brown studied him a moment. "Come here and give grandma a hug."

Carlos ambled into her old wrinkled arms.

"If I can help you, son…you let me know," she said, lifting his chin.

Carlos nodded with a sigh, tried to smile at Grandma Brown and headed out the door for the store.

"Well, well. If it isn't lover boy," Tobias scoffed as Carlos slinked toward him in the cramped corner grocery.

Carlos peered sheepishly at his best friend in the world and choked out, "I need to talk.

$\oint$

Upper West Side

"Really, Cobi," Abby said, "you didn't need to escort me all the way to my door. I do this alone all the time."

Cobi made a face – half frown, half grin. "I've been wanting to talk since we got back from LA. The time just never seemed right."

Cobi paid the driver, slid out of the cab and held the door for Abby to get out. Standing in front of the Majestic apartments, Cobi fidgeted with the coins in his pocket.

"Could I come in for a while? It's important."

Abby studied him. "Nana's out of town for a couple days. She wouldn't want me to have someone up when she's gone."

Cobi nodded, grimacing. "I understand. Maybe another time."

He turned back for a cab but Abby reached for his arm. "Wait. Maybe just for a few minutes."

The doorman's raised eyebrow was not lost on Abby when they reached the entrance. But from his little smirk, she knew he wouldn't say anything – he was like a loving uncle to her.

"Evening, Eddie," Abby offered, trying to appear nonchalant as he held the door. "This is my friend, Cobi. We play together…in a band."

Cobi smiled and nodded at Eddie.

"Cobi, nice to meet you," Eddie said, along with an exaggerated salute. "You are so lucky to know this sweet girl."

Abby looked to the heavens then back to Eddie. "Thank you. *You* are sweet to say that."

Eddie volleyed back, "I know. Say hi to your Grandma for me."

"Eddie…" Abby frowned at the doorman. "I will," and pulled Cobi through the door and in to the elevator.

"What was that about?" Cobi asked, as they were heading up to Nana's floor. "Felt like I was watching a tennis match without knowing the score."

Abby scrunched her face. "He's just looking out for me. I think Nana might have mentioned something to him."

The elevator whooshed open to a richly paneled hall and soft sconce lighting.

Once inside the apartment, Abby turned to lock the door and Cobi continued down the marble hallway to the carpeted living room and stared out the window. "What an amazing view of the park. Looks so quiet at night."

Abby came up and hooked her arm in his. "Alright. What's so important?"

Cobi stretched his neck like he was loosening up for a match. "I…," he stopped and heaved a long breath. "Since LA I've thought a lot about you."

Abby unhooked her arm and stared out the window next to him.

"I know you wanted to get away from Blake because of him and Jaz living together."

She couldn't help but groan.

"And I know we were just friends then…Abby." Cobi put his hand up and scrubbed his forehead. "Could we sit down?"

His sincerity touched her. She took his hand and led him to the couch.

"Is it possible we could go out...together...just the two of us?" he continued with a hopeful sideways grin. "I mean, to have time alone without the whole band around?"

What a sweetheart, Abby thought. "Yes. I would like that," she said and, cupping his face, gave him a kiss.

Cobi hesitated – seemingly to gather courage. He then reached for Abby's waist and held her for a moment peering into her eyes. Abby waited. But not for long. Cobi pulled her in close and kissed her on the neck. Abby shivered and they fell into a clutch. As they leaned back to lie down on the couch, the sound of a key in a lock echoed from the end of the hall.

Chinatown

Travis was beginning to hyperventilate. He had never *officially* met the parents of a girlfriend before. Really, he only had two others that he could have called girlfriends, but that was in the projects and everyone knew your business so there was no need – parents already knew who you were.

"Travis, you're crushing my hand," Mia said as they were coming up from the Canal Street subway station. "Relax. I've timed this so Pa won't be home and I've already told Ma about you."

"You tell her everything."

"You mean that you're beautiful and can play any instrument made out of metal?"

Travis scoffed. "I'm not good at rejection. It's happened."

Mia jumped in front of him and put her hands up to stop him. "I don't care what happens. Nothing will change how I feel about you." She reached up for his neck and pulled his head down for a kiss.

Travis peered side to side after she let him go.

"What's wrong with you, Travis? Ashamed of me?"

He drew in a long breath. Then let it out – slowly. "Doesn't anything bother you?"

"Nope. Now come on, let's get this over with." She grabbed his hand and led him the rest of the block to the Hong Kong Garden restaurant – Travis appearing stricken.

38
Purpose – Saturday, January 29th

"**W**ell, with two weeks to go I think we're in pretty good shape for the fundraiser," Mike said gazing around at *La Familia* spread out on the small back corner stage of the Café, snowflakes lazily fluttering down outside the front window.

Jaz slowly raised her hand. "Actually, Blake and I would like to add kind of a tribute to R.G. No big deal. About three minutes."

Mike was pleased they would think of that. But mixed in was a bit of sadness. "That would be great. Just the two of you?"

"It is for now. But, whatever you think. We know how you like to collaborate," she said with a crooked smile.

"Let's have a listen and see what happens."

Thinking back on their conversations with R.G. (mostly he talked they listened), Jaz and Blake used his life story as inspiration to render a soulful but hopeful musical tribute to his career: how he struggled to make a go of it without a father in his life; his mother dying giving birth to his sister; his bloody beating in a civil rights demonstration; and going blind at thirty-two with only a saxophone to make a living.

How after all that trouble and sadness he was able to play such sweet music in a way that reached the heart – because he believed his gift was God-given and had a purpose. 'Twas a matter of sharing love,' he had told them. 'I loved playing. And folks loved to listen. Don't get no better than that.' At the time they pretty much blew him off. Now, they were beginning to understand.

When Jaz and Blake had finished their tribute, Mike had to turn away to wipe his eyes. He wasn't the only one.

"You two have done me in," Mike said, struck with a wave of gratitude. "I'm thinking you've given us more to consider for our performance."

Mike glanced around at the band. "Any ideas from you guys?"

They all started talking at once. "Yeah, okay. Thought you might," he said raising his hands. "Take some time to swap ideas with Jaz and Blake and see what more you come up with."

It seemed the kids had learned the power and value of their music. It was not just a means to make a living, but a way to reach the hearts of folks – substantial. That was R.G.'s legacy.

Mike thought back on the first time he met R.G. He had just gotten off the subway from playing at Johnny's and was drawn to the mellow lament of a sax coming from the far end of the station platform. Music so exquisite words could not describe but his heart understood. As he walked up to the last support pillar, a white cane leaning against it, he saw R.G. with his sax case laying open for tips. Thank God he convinced R.G. to play with his band at the Central Park Concert, which had launched Mike's career as a composer.

After a couple of hours, with Mike sitting at the Café bar writing out ideas and notations of his own, he pulled tables together in front of the stage and gathered everyone around to hear what they had came up with.

"I don't know if we'll have enough time for all the ideas," Blake said, looking wild-eyed.

"I bet we can. Remember, we had less than ten days to learn all new music for the Radio City performance."

As the kids batted around ideas, Naomi walked in with four boxes of warm carryout – Noah running ahead for hugs and high-fives.

Mike stood, grabbed his son and lifted him up. "Okay, everyone, time for lunch."

Pizza, teenagers and a common purpose – couldn't get any better.

After Naomi and Noah finished their pizza, they headed upstairs and Mike moved to his perch at the far end of the coffee bar to give the kids some space – not hovering. However, he had learned to read them pretty well by the tone of their voices and body language. Sneaking a glance now and then while reading *Variety*, he was able to keep up to date on the latest drama.

$$\textit{\clef treble}$$

Jaz stood from the table and picked up Blake's plate when she saw he had finished. "Want the same or something different?"

Blake looked at her, puzzled. "Ah…I'll try the pineapple and ham."

"You sure? Looks disgusting," she said smiling – not with her usual edge.

"Yeah, it's good. You should try it."

Jaz shrugged, "Okay. Why not?" and stepped over to the pizza boxes putting two slices on his plate. As she ambled back to him, she had an uncharacteristic softness about her. Blake reached for his plate and peered up at her – enamored.

Abby's eyes narrowed taking in the exchange between Blake and Jaz and turned her head away as she leaned back.

Cobi bent over and nudged her. "What?"

Abby swung her head back to him. "Oh…nothing."

"Nothing?"

Cobi wasn't sure where he stood with Abby, but things could have gotten a lot hotter if her grandmother hadn't come home early from her trip. But then, catching what was going on at the next table, he realized what had upset Abby. Was Blake trying to make her jealous or was it over between them? Cobi *really* didn't care for being a pawn in their little chess game. He needed to have words with Blake, and soon.

𝄞

Tobias got up from the table and nodded to Carlos to follow him to the other end of the bar from Mike. They sat down on stools facing each other.

"Been thinking about your…um…dilemma with Sophia. I've heard girls sometimes fake being pregnant to get a guy to commit. Especially a good Catholic boy like you."

"I don't know," Carlos mumbled. "She seemed pretty sure."

"Pretty sure of what?" Tobias's voice raised. "Getting you to marry her?"

Carlos slumped and peered around. "Shut up would you." Then he leaned on the bar with his head in his hands.

"Look," Tobias whispered. "I don't want to hear about you getting married until you're sure she's…"

Carlos moaned. "Shit. How can this be happening? It was only one time."

𝄞

Mia had it with Travis. Either they were going together or not. When she came back with a plate piled with four slices of pizza, instead of setting it in from of him, she wormed her way onto his lap and started feeding him. Travis just closed his eyes like he wanted to disappear. When he opened them and looked around, no one noticed or cared. It seemed everyone knew what was going on before he was even sure.

𝄞

After witnessing all the drama bubbling around him, Mike needed to get with Naomi. Maybe she would have insight on how to counsel the kids. But, now that they had come up with a theme for the fundraiser, R.G.'s legacy, he wanted to encourage their collaboration and see what they came up with. He got their commitment to practice the next six Saturdays. And, yes, it would be all original music.

39
Inspiration

After arranging chairs and music stands to accommodate *La Familia* in the apartment living room, Mike slipped behind Naomi in the kitchen and hugged her as she stood at the stove.

"I love you," Mike said. "Not many wives would have eight teenage misfits take over her home for weeks."

Naomi twisted to look at him. "This is only until the fundraiser…right?"

"Of course. Unless you find you can't live without them hanging around up here."

She turned back to the stove with a snort.

"It will enable us to get in more practice in the afternoons while keeping the Café open from lunch 'til the evening crowd."

Naomi lowered the flame under the pot of soup she'd been working on and turned to him. "You do realize you can't keep them from making mistakes. Unfortunately, it's how we learn sometimes what *not* to do. The best *we* can do is set a good example."

Mike moaned. "I know. Just hate to see them get hurt."

Naomi held his face with both hands. "We have both survived great hurt – it's unavoidable. I think they know by now we are there for them."

Naomi reminded Mike that she needed to pick up Noah from his morning acting class at The Children's Acting Academy then stop in to visit Rose in Harlem.

"They love him there, saying he's the total package – acts, sings and dances like a little pro. The trouble is…he now thinks he doesn't need to do his regular studies," Naomi said.

"Sure you still want to homeschool him? Maybe we should look into a private school."

"I'm not sure we could afford it right now. Let's finish out the year where he is and see how that goes," Naomi said, pulling on her coat. "For now I just want to be his mama."

Mike headed downstairs with her to hail a cab. Just as they got to the curb, Jaz and Blake pulled up in a taxi.

"Mr. and Mrs. M," Jaz shouted, as she slid out from the back seat with Blake right behind, grinning ear-to-ear.

Jaz was beaming. "You guys are early," Mike said, hardly recognizing the grinning girl.

"Can't wait to show you what more we've come up with."

Mike just shook his head. It wasn't long ago that Jaz claimed she had no interest in composing.

"Head upstairs. I'll be up in a minute."

After sending Naomi off to pick up Noah, Mike hung out by the door to greet the rest of the group. It thrilled him to watch as the kids experienced the magic of creating art – like stepping into another dimension leaving behind the real world and all its challenges, if only for a while.

With everyone spread out like in the "practice closet" at the Y, Mike hardly knew where to begin. "Wow! Here we are again."

Mike looked each of them in the eyes then continued. "Seems we've been blessed with a win-win opportunity here: to use your gift of making music to raise funds to help build a school for the Liberian orphanage; but, we also win don't we. We get to create music that not only honors our good friend R.G. but also challenges us all to grow. Do you remember how upset you were when I suggested we compose music for the Radio City competition? Yet you trusted me, if begrudgingly. That meant a lot to me. Just a warning though, it won't be any easier just because we did it once. It will take just as much blood, sweat and tears, but, God willing in the end we will do R.G. proud." Mike could feel the energy building in the room. *Better get started before they explode.*

Mike heaved a great sigh, walked over to the wall behind Blake and continued. "I bought this rolling chalkboard to help us in outlining R.G.'s opus." He pushed it in front of the group then handed out notebooks to each of them. "Keep the notebooks with you at all times because you never know when inspiration might strike. You don't want to take the chance of losing a good idea. The big board will be updated regularly with the latest infusion of ideas."

Mike reached for a piece of chalk and started writing a column on the left of the eight-foot chalkboard. "This will be our "To Do" list that will help us stay focused. Since we agreed R.G.'s life is our inspiration, we will decide on the various movements and who will be working on each of them." Mike paused. "Any questions so far?"

Jaz raised her hand with her usual smirk. "Who decides who works on what part?"

Mike knew this was coming. "At first its wide open. Work on what ever inspires you. I'm thinking it will become clear what works and what doesn't after we hear what bubbles up from each of you. But, in the end, one of us will have to decide." Mike finished his little repartee with a syrupy smile.

"And that person would be you...I take it?" Jaz added.

"Bingo," Mike replied. "I still have a *little* more experience on you all, but you're closing in fast."

Cobi, seemingly unable to sit still another minute, let out a brief frenzied drum roll ending with a crash of the cymbal. "Sorry. But are we going to play something soon. This is beginning to feel like school."

Mike smiled. "Sorry Cobi, you're right. I'll turn it over to Blake and Jaz. Appears they've got something to share with you. We'll see how it fits in later."

Blake, having taken piano lessons for most his life, had written out scores for the other instruments to enhance the sketch they played for the group at the Café.

Mike rolled the chalkboard back against the wall to get it out of their way and started writing an outline for the week.

It struck Mike, as he outlined the progression of the composition, how similar R.G.'s story was to Sarah Davis's, the inspiration for his Broadway hit *The Girl in the Yellow Scarf*. How early in their life they were influenced by people of faith that got them through soul crushing loss of family and then having to survive on their own. Sarah had her Grandma Mae and R.G. had a pastor who ministered to him while R.G. was in prison for possession of illegal drugs. Once again, as in his other compositions, a recurring theme was needed to tie the composition together from beginning to end. He wasn't quite sure where to go with Noah representing that theme. But he'd learned to let the idea marinate for a while and trust that it would become clear with time.

Closing in on six o'clock, they needed to shut down the music-making machine to get back to reality and their "day" jobs. All but Travis, Blake and Jaz headed downstairs to get ready for the Saturday evening crowd. Mike could see their reluctance to return to their blue-collar jobs and knew firsthand how that felt. But, in a way, it made their time creating all the sweeter.

After he was left alone Mike continued to outline his thoughts for the composition. In a way, it seemed to follow the circle of life: how we enter this world a clean slate then what we experience shapes and molds us and if we are lucky there are folks in our lives that teach us how to live a good life, one of value and purpose. This was certainly true for Sarah and R.G. As Mike was finishing up the outline, Noah streaked in and slammed into him, joyfully, bringing him back to the present.

"Papa, guess what I did today?" Noah said, flying at about 20,000 feet.

Mike put his hand to his chin and scrubbed it. "Let's see. You got up, went to the bathroom, brushed your teeth then came downstairs for breakfast. Then –"

Noah wasn't having his little joke and drilled into Mike with an expression like he'd chomped into a slice of lemon.

"No, Papa, that's boring stuff. I got ta perform today." The sour look was instantly replaced with one of joy. "They told me I could do what I wanted. So…I made a story 'bout Curly and me livin' in da forest in Africa. We made friends with forest animals and slept in a big bird nest high in a tree to be safe from mean hunters lookin' for us. It was a little sad but fun and it made da teacher cry."

Mike looked at Naomi – *incredible.*

Naomi said, "I can fill you in later. But for now this boy needs a bath then some time with his homework. Seems he needs to be able to read if he wants to become an actor some day. Imagine that."

"Reading's a good idea. Can we work some math in there and maybe writing out these fantasy stories of his?"

"I see where you're going," Naomi said. "By the way, how did you do at math?"

"Think you know the answer to that. Just look at my checkbook."

"That reminds me. We need to talk finances tonight. You've been putting that off for a week now."

Mike cringed and gave Naomi a nod then grabbed his boy for a trip up the stairs and bath time.

After a late dinner and reading a bedtime story, Mike sat and watched his "jungle" boy fall asleep while on the last page of the book. The sweet spirit of his child was evident even as he slept. Thinking of how insistent the Y kids were on having Noah be part of the opus, a welling of emotion suddenly hit him. After everything this boy had been through in his first six years of life, resilience remained. Maybe, Mike thought, Noah could represent the unbroken spirit that was present throughout R.G.'s life, enabling him to survive in spite of everything that tried to bring him down. Noah and the soul quenching way he plays his recorder could represent the spirit of God that dwells in all of us. But it's still up to us to allow that spirit to guide us – as R.G. most certainly did. He didn't have to say a word. You could feel it in his music.

After kissing his sleeping boy Mike headed downstairs, buoyed by a sense of purpose he hadn't felt since creating *The Girl* opus. But this would be different. Even better. Sharing the joy of creating with his treasured students.

The four weeks leading up to the benefit concert at Harlem Baptist had all the drama of a daytime soap opera with a dash of romantic comedy thrown in. Without Naomi to help Mike unravel the mysteries of teenage histrionics he was sure he would have gone mad – mistakenly thinking it was only composing an opus that needed sorting out. In spite of the turbulence that swirled beneath each practice session, they had accomplished their goal – *Lost and Found*, a musical tribute to their friend and hero R.G.

"Can you believe it?" Mike asked the kids spread out for practice in the apartment living room. "I think we've got it."

"Hey, no sweat," Cobi chimed in from behind his drums. "Well, maybe some sweat and a little blood," he said holding up a bandaged finger. "But at least I didn't shed tears unlike someone I know," he said smirking at Mike.

"Hey, those were tears of joy," Mike said, defending his reaction to hearing Jaz and Blake's early tribute sketch to R.G.

"Sure…whatever," Cobi said, as the rest of the kids grinned sympathetically at him.

"Okay, time to get back to work. Soon as Noah comes in from feeding Curly out back we'll go through it non-stop one last time."

Mike couldn't have been happier with how the kids collaborated in composing the six-movement opus inspired by R.G.'s extraordinary life. Starting with growing up on the mean streets of South Bronx and raised by a single mother that made sure he was cared for in mind, body and spirit – seeing that his school work was always done, he was fed and clothed and accompanied her to church each Sunday. His mother's early nurturing would remain with him but couldn't shield him from a cruel world that seemed out to get him. After a brief opening section of popular music from R.G.'s time, the first movement titled *Mother's Love* introduced R.G.'s indomitable spirit, portrayed by the simple serene quality of Noah's recorder. This musical theme of sustaining love would reappear throughout the remaining four movements – sometimes struggling to be heard over the tumult of violence, prejudice and addiction that would haunt him.

Waiting for Noah to get back from feeding his dog, the kids were beginning to get restless.

"Would one of you please go out and tell that boy to get in here? He's holding us up!" Mike said, impatiently.

Travis was the first to jump up. "He'll listen to me, Mr. M."

Mike knew Travis was a favorite of Noah's. They seemed to have a lot in common, learning early in life to make it on their own.

With Mike busy getting the kids ready for their concert, Naomi finally took time off from overseeing the Café now that they had hired an alternate manager to fill in for her and Mia. It wasn't often she had the day to herself but, after some shopping, she ended up in Harlem to see Rose. Having no surviving family of her own, Mike's mother and siblings had become a treasure to her and she loved spending time with them.

"I can hardly stand not seeing that sweet boy every day," Rose said, as they sat together on the living room couch. "I just might have to move in with you all for awhile."

"That would be fine with me," Naomi replied. "But your fiancé might object."

"Oh yeah...him. But we won't be married for another six weeks."

"Great. I'll help you pack. I could use some help getting that child to finish his schoolwork. It's hard to pull him out of his imaginary world. I often find him play-acting with Curly in some new adventure either in the attic studio or in the backyard. I suspect you've had experience with someone like that."

"I think I could write a book on ways to get a creative child through school. That boy of yours sure takes after his father," Rose said with a far off look. "Probably could have saved Michael a lot of pain, as well as his father and me, if I had recognized his gift sooner. Going to Cornell to get a business degree to please his parents practically killed him."

Naomi slid over on the couch to put her arm around Rose. "Your big boy has turned out just fine. Thank you for giving him what he needed most. Your love."

Rose put her head on Naomi's shoulder and sighed.

"Why don't you come to the Café with me?" Naomi asked, turning to smile at her mother-in-law. "You could get a preview of what they're working on."

Rose brightened and jumped up to get her coat. "Great idea. I've got a batch of cookies I can take for the kids."

The day was exceptionally sunny and warm for February as Rose and Naomi stood arm-in-arm at the curb waiting for their cab. It didn't seem the day could get much better.

As Naomi and Rose were coming in the front door to the apartment stairs, Travis ran in from the back door meeting them in the hall. Travis stopped in front of them looking horrified – holding Noah's recorder with Curly whimpering in his arms.

41

Lost

When Travis didn't show up with Noah Mike sensed something was wrong. He told the group to take five and headed downstairs trying hard not to show he was upset. When he walked into the Café from the apartment hallway he saw Naomi drooped in a chair with Noah's recorder on the table in front of her. His mother and Travis ran in from the street appearing frantic. Mike rushed to Naomi trying to sort out what was going on. She looked up at him with a look of rage he'd never seen in her. Before he could get a word out she sprung up and lunged at him.

"Mike…he's…gone," she stammered and started pounding on his chest. "You were supposed to be watching him!"

He stumbled back trying to deflect her blows. "What…gone?"

Naomi wailed with her head back then slumped to the floor retching with sobs.

Rose ran to Naomi, crouched down and rocked her as she sobbed. Mike looked on bewildered, trying to make sense of it.

Mike protested. "He's not gone," and ran past Travis knocking over chairs to get to the alley.

He leaped off the back stoop. Blind with terror, he crashed into a garbage can and went sprawling onto the asphalt alley. His arms and knees bloodied, he sprang up and ran up and down cranking his head side-to-side yelling for his son. Mike ended his search at the back entrance to the Café where Travis stood holding Curly – pain etched on his face.

"Mr. M...I've looked everywhere."

"He couldn't just disappear," Mike shouted and charged past Travis.

When every corner of the apartment and Café had been searched, Mike, his mother and Naomi sat huddled around a table waiting for the police to arrive. The kids were sent home and the closed sign was hung on the Café door.

$$\oint$$

Hunched under a tattered blanket, Noah sat shivering but stoic on a filthy mattress. Marcus stood watch, peering out one of the few unbroken windows of the burned-out five-story high rise. He turned and walked up to Noah. "Collin should be back with the burgers soon, but in the meantime, I want to ask you about your *new* dad."

Noah turned his head away and looked across the room.

Marcus reached down and backhanded Noah. "Look at me when I'm talking."

The blow was numbing at first then started to throb. Noah slowly turned to face Marcus with a blank stare.

"That's better. Don't think I won't throw you off the roof if you don't listen to me."

Noah began to pant, but tried to tamp down his fear as he stared at Marcus.

"This could be over soon if your folks come up with the two-hundred grand. Seems your grandpa, the professor, used the grant money he came into for his own purpose. Anyway, shouldn't be a problem for your dad to raise the cash, being a famous composer and all."

𝄞

After getting the call about the missing child, a sergeant from the 10th precinct got to the Café within minutes. He explained that in cases of missing children the first three hours are most critical. He hurriedly wrote down a description of Noah and grabbed his photos. As he rushed to leave he turned back from the door. "Know that we'll do everything possible to find your boy. The best thing you can do is stay by the phone in case we need more information." A sudden pall of helplessness overtook Mike.

As he sat across from Naomi and his mother after the sergeant left, Mike twitched with anxiety. "I need to check with Rudy. Maybe he can help. He had twenty years on the force."

His mother reached for his hand to stop him. "We'll stay by the phone till you get back but before you go we need to pray."

𝄞

As soon as Rudy saw Mike walk up to the bar at Johnny's he left his customer mid-sentence and hustled over. "My god, Mike, you look terrible. What's going on?"

Mike explained what happened, filling in every detail he could think of: time of day Noah went missing; what he was wearing; friends of his; and then answered a dozen other questions. Satisfied he'd gotten every possible stitch of information, Rudy looked Mike hard in the eye. "This is not a time to fall into old habits. Getting drunk isn't going to solve this."

Mike had to admit he was tempted. "I know."

Rudy nodded. "I'm all over this Mike. I'll not rest till everything possible is done."

Mike sagged with his elbows on the bar. "Rudy…thank you."

Mike knew it was probably fruitless but he couldn't help himself. After leaving Johnny's, he hailed a cab and had him drive up and down the streets and avenues of Chelsea – scanning the crowds for a glimpse of his son. After a futile hour the driver dropped him off at the Café. He stood staring into the front window knowing there was nothing more he could do – thankful for Mother's prayer and Rudy's determination.

When Mike walked in, he was immediately met with a hug from the Reverend. Mike clung to him as his knees trembled.

"Mike, the whole church is praying," the Reverend whispered in his ear. Holding Mike out by the shoulders, he continued. "For now, the plan for the benefit is put on hold… until we get him back."

Mike tried to smile but wasn't successful. "Where are Naomi and Mother?"

"Upstairs. I'm concerned about Naomi though. She's practically catatonic with dread. You better go up and be with her."

Mike entered their bedroom to only a dim glow from a lamp next to where his mother sat humming. She got up to hug and kiss him on the cheek, then headed downstairs. Mike crept to the edge of the bed and looked down at his bride.

She slowly rolled her head to look at him. "I thought we would be safe here."

Mike had no answer to that.

"My heart is…split open," she said between shallow breaths. Then, with a gasp, "I can't lose him, too…"

Mike tried to think of something comforting, but could only lie next to her and hold her hand. *Dear God, give me strength.*

𝄞

When Collin got back with the burgers, Marcus was on him immediately. "Where the *hell* you been?"

Collin threw the bag of burgers across the room at Marcus. "Had a lot to do, man. Made arrangements for the boat, made the call to the Monroe's and got your dinner. What you been doin?"

"Don't forget, none of this was possible without me," Marcus snarled, digging into the fast-food bag. After chomping into a double burger with everything he peered over at Noah – still as a marble statue with the blanket up to his chin. "Want something kid?"

Noah's eyes shifted to drill into Marcus.

"I said…do you want something?"

Noah didn't budge.

Marcus groaned. "Forget it you little shit."

Collin picked up an empty beer can from the table and threw it at Marcus. "You freakin' bully. He's just a kid. Give him a burger."

Marcus batted the can away and drew his .38 special tucked in the back of his pants. "Don't do that again."

Collin just grinned and unzipped his jacket to show his holstered 9mm Glock. "You got a gun alright. But I've got a boat and a gun. And my gun packs more punch."

Marcus snorted, tucking his gun in his belt. "We can debate that another time. What was the response to your call?"

"Of course he said he didn't have it. But he came around when I told him he had 24 hours if he wanted his son back."

"Sure you can ditch anyone following you tomorrow?"

"I know Times Square. Just drive to where you're supposed to be after you secure the kid here. I'll find my way to you after shaking anyone that might be following me. Then the boat to Jersey and Newark airport."

Noah listened to the whole scheme. Collin would leave in the morning to prepare for the money drop. Then Marcus would meet him later with the car. It seemed Collin was looking out for Noah and didn't want him hurt but Noah didn't trust Marcus. Noah feared that after Collin left in the morning, Marcus wouldn't leave Noah behind – alive. Why would he? Collin could easily disappear with his share of the money but Marcus was headed back to Liberia where he could be tracked down. Noah needed to escape – tonight.

42

Bargain

Still in his clothes, Mike woke next to Naomi and was immediately slammed with foreboding. It was still dark with rumbling off in the distance from an approaching storm. Naomi moaned and turned to him.

"What happens now?"

Somehow he had to be strong. But all he could think of was to get up and move – do something – anything.

"Rudy knows we can't come up with the whole two-hundred thousand, so he suggested we get what we can and he'll take care of stretching it to look like the whole amount."

Naomi tried to push herself up to sit but fell back on the pillow. "Stretch it?"

"He has access to dummy one-hundred dollar bills and currency bands to fill twenty $10,000 bundles. The genuine hundreds will go on top. I'll go to the bank for the eight thousand in our saving account and get with Rudy."

"If..." Naomi pulled her hands to her face, "if they fall for that, how do we get our son back. Where are they keeping him?"

"The guy on the phone said after he gets the money he'll call and give us the address to where to find him. He is safe and unharmed." Mike wasn't sure why but felt he could trust the guy.

"Mike," Naomi said, shaking her head, "why Noah? He's only been here a few months."

"Don't know. Rudy says kidnapping for ransom is usually done by someone who knows the family. I didn't recognize anything about the guy on the phone."

Naomi grabbed Mike's hand, as he was about to get out of bed. "As soon as you know where he is…you come and get me. Understood?"

Mike wasn't sure what he was in for and didn't want her along in case there was trouble. "Rudy will be involved in getting him but I suppose –"

"Suppose! You just come and get me." Naomi lurched up in bed and scowled at him.

"Okay, yes, of course."

𝄞

Marcus came in from the other room when it was time for him to leave and kicked Noah's mattress. "Well kid, it's just you and me now." Not getting any response he kicked the mattress harder. "Get up, dammit!"

The covers didn't move. Marcus bent over and ripped back the blanket finding only a rolled up sleeping bag and peeled duct tape from Noah's hands and ankles. The covers were still warm.

𝄞

Mike wasn't sure he could hold it together. With maybe an hour of sleep his nerves were jangling and his chest ached. Rudy had contacted a couple plainclothes detectives that would shadow Mike throughout the ordeal. When he got the call to deliver the money to a location in Times Square, Mike headed up to let Naomi know he was leaving. He tried his best to appear confident that all would end well – despite the odds.

Naomi gasped when she saw him walk in. She was sitting up in bed trying to eat some toast from a tray Rose had brought her.

"Rudy just pulled up out front. He's got a plan…"

"Hope it brings him home," Naomi's voice trailed off. She pushed the tray away and lay down to face the alley window.

𝄞

Marcus had Noah's shoes so he knew he wouldn't get far with all the rubble and broken glass that went on for blocks and blocks in the burned out apartments. He stuffed his .38 in his belt under his shirt, pulled up his hood and headed out for a little game of hide-and-seek.

𝄞

Mike got in the unmarked police car idling out front of the Café and sat in the front seat swaying like he was teetering on the edge of a cliff.

"Mike, I would do this for you if I could. But you're the only one that can, " Rudy said. "I can't image what you're feeling."

Mike gulped a huge breath. "I just want to kill the guy. I'm afraid when I see him I'll go for his throat and strangle him."

"Mike!" Rudy slammed his hand on the steering wheel. "That won't get Noah back."

Mike grabbed the edge of the seat with both hands trying to control his rage.

"We'll try our best to track the guy after he has the money… but it sounds like he knows what he's doing. So after the drop, an officer will get you home for the call and take you to pick up your boy."

Mike slowly turned to look Rudy in the eye hoping for some reassurance. But what he saw wasn't what Mike hoped for – a thin veneer of confidence covering grave concern.

43
Hide-and-Seek

After a quick search of the other rooms on the fifth floor, Marcus went up to the roof and walked the perimeter. He scanned as far as he could see – the crumbling burned out buildings that once housed thousands. The kid couldn't have gotten far; he only left Noah for a few minutes so he could take a leak. He leaned over the edge of the roof now and then as he ambled along but only saw a mangy mutt tugging at something in the burned out carcass of a car. He pulled out his .38 and took aim. He was a good shot but the dog was a little out of range. If he had his M16 he used back in Liberia– no problem.

When Noah heard Marcus' scuffling overhead he leapt from the fire escape through the broken out fourth floor window. Fortunately, Marcus decided to go up to the roof instead of down to check out the other floors. Unfortunately, Noah had stepped on a rusty spike that went clear through his foot. Gritting his teeth, he yanked his foot from the board with the nail and wrapped the wound with a piece of rag he found. But blood eventually soaked through, leaving a trail of bloody splotches.

♪

Marcus couldn't wait to get out of this country and back to the revolution. But first he needed to find and bury that kid. He jogged down the steps to the fourth floor and started searching the rooms. "Come on, kid," he called out. "It's time to go. We'll stop and pick up some burgers on the way to get Collin."

He came to a window and looked out onto the fire escape. Then he noticed fresh blood on the windowsill and blotches across the room leading out to the stairs.

♪

When Noah reached the third floor he looked back up the stairs and saw a trail of his blood. He ran into the next room and tore off his shirt and wrapped his foot twice around – making a knot with the sleeves. He then scurried to the open window and lunged through it onto the metal grate of the fire escape just as Marcus was thumping down the stairs. Marcus followed the blood to where the trail stopped in the middle of the apartment bedroom. He looked up as if Noah might be hanging from the light fixture. Scowling at his own stupidity, he pulled out the .38 from his belt and headed for the fire escape window. The only place Noah could have gone.

44
Shadow and Light

Mike stared aimlessly out the patrol car windshield waiting until they would head to Times Square. Often when he felt low, Sarah Davis would come to mind – the one who helped get him past debilitating guilt over his father's death and set him on a path to his career saving opus, *The Girl in the Yellow Scarf*. Besides her incredible life story and voice, that inspired his composition, she was also an amazing artist. Once, when he had fallen into a dark mood, she reached to cup his face with her small soft hands. 'You need both shadow *and* light to make a drawing come alive. Kind of like life; where there is shadow there is also light…if we look for it.' She could make a drawing come off the page.

"Mike…time to go."

Mike turned to Rudy. "What?"

"It's time."

𝄞

Collin stood across the street from Times Square watching to see if Mike would come alone. He had observed Mike for the last week at The Opus Café to get a feel for the guy. He had to admit this kind of gig wasn't his favorite but if Mike didn't do anything stupid he would get his kid back and everyone could go on about their lives. Five minutes to twelve he watched Mike walk up 46th street and wait in front of the bus stop where he was told to hand off the money. When Collin saw the bus coming a block away he headed across the street to the bus stop weaving through the noontime crowd. When it arrived he cut in line to get on the bus and headed for one of the rear seats. As the bus idled, waiting for the light to turn green, a kid in a hoody bumped into Mike, stuffed a note in his hand and hustled off into the crowd. Mike read the short note and lurched to the bus and pounded on the passenger door. The driver glared at him but opened the door and Mike jumped on just as the light turned green. After handing off his fare, he walked to the last seat on the bus and slid in next to the window like the note said. Two stops later Mike got off, leaving the small backpack on the rear seat floor. As soon as Mike got up and headed down the aisle to the front Collin slid over from his seat and casually stuffed the small backpack into a large shopping bag. A couple stops later Collin got off with his Macy's bag and headed into St. Paddy's Bar to wait for Marcus.

$$\oint$$

Before Marcus stuck his head out the fourth floor window looking for Noah, Noah was able to hobble down the fire escape to the next level. But when he got there both windows to the third floor were jammed closed. All he could do was climb onto the windowsill recess and press against the glass hoping Marcus wouldn't catch sight of him. But Marcus crawled out the window onto the fire escape and looked down through the metal grate. If it wasn't for the wad of shirt wrapped around Noah's foot he might have headed back inside.

"Ah…there you are. You're making us late getting to Collin," he said with a smirk and made his way down the metal steps to Noah. When he got to the third floor platform and was about to reach the kid, Noah grunted and drove both his elbows into the window with everything he had. The glass shattered with him falling back into the room along with jagged shards. Marcus stepped to the window and looked in. Noah was lying on his back bleeding from deep gashes in his bare arms and legs.

"Well now. Appears you don't have much time before you run out of blood…and I didn't even have to touch you." Marcus turned around to check if anyone might have wandered on the scene below. He snorted with the thought. There was no one within blocks. "Got to hand it to you kid. You're tough. But you should have stayed in Africa. It's not safe here."

Marcus almost felt sorry for Noah, watching him bleed out on the floor. But as he was reaching into his jacket for a cigarette, Noah let out a primal scream from the bottom of his soul and sprang to his feet. He charged through the broken out window catching Marcus off balance – sending them both over the railing of the fire escape.

$\oint$

When Marcus was over an hour late getting to St. Paddy's, Collin figured something had gone wrong. He would have to fall back on plan B to get out of New York on his own. But leaving the kid tied up in the Bronx gnawed on him. So, before he checked into the nearest flophouse, he called Mike from a pay phone to tell him where his kid was.

$\oint$

When the phone rang it seemed to shred Mike's last nerve. He shook so bad he could barely hold the receiver to his ear. He listened to the brief message, put down the phone and motioned to Naomi. "Let's go get him." She stood from sitting on the bed and stumbled into his arms.

Rudy was waiting for them when they came downstairs to the Café. He could see Naomi was about to come undone so he ran up to help her to the car waiting out front.

When they got to the burned-out projects in South Bronx they could only get within a hundred yards of where Noah was supposed to be held because of all the debris and abandon cars strewn around. The two patrol cars that were following pulled to a stop in a line behind Rudy. Climbing through the rubble the team of four officers surrounded the building while Mike and Rudy walked to the front of the crumbling building arm-in-arm with Naomi who had refused to stay in the car.

"Noah!" hollered Naomi, as they entered the first floor, stepping around stained mattresses and broken furniture. Mike and Rudy joined in calling Noah's name as they went room to room. When they reached the back of the first floor apartment Naomi froze as she looked out the rear window. Lying on the caved in roof of an abandoned Chevy was Marcus on his back – with Noah sprawled on top of him – blood dripping through the busted out windshield, puddled on the instrument panel.

Naomi's knees buckled. Rudy hung on keeping her from falling while Mike scrambled out the back door to get to the car. He jumped onto the hood and clambered on all fours to reach his bleeding son. He gradually pulled Noah off Marcus' crushed body and fell back onto the hood, enfolding Noah in his arms. Mike's mouth fell open to scream but only sobs retched from his chest. Rudy spun around with Naomi to get to his car, while two officers ran to their car, leaving the other officers to deal with Marcus' body.

Naomi waited in the back seat with the door open as Mike stumbled close behind cradling Noah, limp in his arms. Reaching Rudy's car, Mike eased Noah into Naomi's open arms and ran panic stricken around to the other door and slid in next to her. After contacting Lincoln Medical ER, four blocks away, Rudy turned around to follow the lead car – sirens wailing. As Mike watched the shallow rise and fall of his son's chest, Noah briefly peered up at him. His son's loving gaze sliced through a dark cloud of hopelessness – shadow and light.

45
Rescue

A gurney was waiting at the ER entrance as Rudy slid to a stop and jumped out to open Naomi's door. She stood slowly, shrouding her son from the grasping arms of hospital staff. Not wanting to let loose of Noah she attempted to lie down on the gurney with him but Mike reached to hold her. "Let's walk next to him."

On the trip to the ER Naomi carefully wiped blood off Noah's face and arms with Mike's jeans jacket that she hugged to her chest as they hustled along with the gurney. Rudy parked the patrol car nearby then headed to the waiting room. When they reached the hall to the examination rooms, with Mike and Naomi clinging to the gurney, a huge but kind orderly motioned for them to stop and find seats in the waiting room. "They need time with him. Please. They'll keep you posted on what's needed."

Mike wanted to barge past the guy but reached for Naomi's shoulders instead and led her to where Rudy stood waiting for them.

"I called Rose. She's on her way," Rudy said, and sat down next to them.

♩

Almost immediately after Noah disappeared down the hall to the ICU a nurse rushed out to ask for volunteer blood donors, preferably O-, the universal blood type. Rudy instantly jumped up to follow the nurse, as did Reverend Robinson who had just arrived. After hours in surgery along with numerous reports from doctors and nurses, the waiting room had swollen to capacity with members of the Monroe family and the Y kids as well as visits from friends at Johnny's and the Opus Café. Finally, going on ten at night, the head surgeon appeared from the hall. Naomi grabbed Mike's arm with both hands as they slowly stood to meet him.

The doc got right to the point. "The blood transfusions helped stabilize him while we were able to deal with his head wound, a fractured femur and multiple cuts. He's not out of the woods...but we're hopeful."

"Can we see him *now*?" Naomi practically shouted.

"Of course."

A nurse led Mike and Naomi to Noah's room, the others staying behind anxiously waiting.

Two nurses were attending Noah when they walked in – a monitor beeped along with oxygen and IV tubes.

Naomi stood with her hands to her face peering down at her bruised and bandaged son. Mike looked for a seat as his knees wobbled. One of the nurses pulled a chair over just as Mike was about to crumble. Mike sat down and lightly held Noah's arm above the IV as Naomi walked to the other side of the bed to a chair waiting for her. If it weren't for the slow beeping of the monitor, Noah was so still it seemed he had already left them.

The doctor had told Mike and Naomi the next few hours were critical so both just sat gazing on their son – praying. The doctor returned after an hour to check Noah's vitals then motioned for them to follow him out to the hall. Smiling, the doctor told them he felt confident their son was going to recover – if slowly. It seemed Noah was sustained by their presence.

Mike immediately grabbed the surgeon for a handshake and headed down the stairs. Seeing all the anxious faces as he came out of the elevator, Mike couldn't help himself. He stumbled to the nearest chair and sat down hard – sobbing with relief.

His people ran over to him gasping and crying. His mother fell to her knees in front of him to hold his dripping face.

"Oh Lord…Michael."

Mike peered up at the horror in his mother's face and tried mightily to gather himself. "Oh…no, no. He's alive! He's going to make it."

Suddenly, the gasps and sobs of heartbreak became gasps and sobs of euphoria. The room exploded into a joy riot – everyone hugging and bouncing around like they'd won the lottery, but even better.

46

Redemption

Peace. Something the Monroe family hadn't experienced for quite awhile. Mike left the Closed sign on the Café door for another few days after bringing Noah home from the hospital. With all the news in the papers of his kidnapping and eventual recovery it was time to shut out the world and be thankful. Only the Y kids were allowed in for practice but it was held downstairs in the Café so as not to excite Noah who was eager to get out of bed.

For Mike, walking in the early March shower that morning was healing – noticing as never before the tender green buds on the trees and bushes – the air moist, reviving – the mist over Washington Square Park, dreamy. After running some errands, Mike burst in their second floor apartment with a dripping umbrella and three bouquets of tulips.

"What's the occasion?" Naomi said, coming to the table with her mid-morning cup of coffee.

"Life. Love. And the pursuit of happiness," Mike said, looking in the kitchen cabinets for vases.

"If I remember right, liberty is in there somewhere?"

"Oh yeah. But love should've been in there, too."

It had been a long time since he'd felt giddy. "What color do you think Noah would like? Yellow, purple or pink?"

"Why don't you take them up and ask him? But, I get what's left over!"

Mike peered at her sideways not sure if she was joking. But her little smirk spoke of love.

Mike put down the flowers and scooted over and hoisted her in the air. "You…you are the sunshine of my life. And that boy? Well…" Mike set her down and had to swallow a sob blooming in his throat.

Naomi wrapped her arms around him and nuzzled his neck. "We've been blessed." After a long embrace Mike heaved a sigh and headed up with the flowers to see his son.

Mike peeked around the open door to catch Noah gazing out the window – Curly snoozing next to him on the bed.

Mike stood there a moment just watching him.

"What are you dreaming about?" Mike said, easing into the room.

Noah turned stiffly to face him. "When can I come downstairs, Papa?"

"In a while." Mike held up the bouquets. "You get to choose first. What's your favorite color?"

Noah studied the flowers for a half minute. "Can I have one from each color?"

Mike smiled. "Good idea. I'll give you some of each." Mike went to Noah's desk and pulled out the wilted flowers from the vase sitting there and put in four of each – yellow, pink and purple.

"Papa," Noah looked at Mike – serious. "Why did Marcus want to kill me?"

Mike's joyous mood instantly vanished. He had to think a moment.

"I don't know for sure. But I'll bet he didn't have much love in his life." Mike decided to leave it at that.

Noah moaned and lay back down. "I feel sorry for him."

Mike didn't know what to say. He stepped over, sat on the edge of the bed and petted Curly, who peered up at Mike, sleepy-eyed.

Mike gave his son a sympathetic smile. "You know if you feel up to it, I think it's time you come downstairs. We need to start getting ready for the fundraiser."

Noah lit up like fireworks. "Papa...can I play the piano for awhile?"

"Think your leg cast might get in the way." Mike watched Noah's face fall. "Hey, we'll figure something out."

Noah nodded with a smile.

"Not sure what Mama will say about you coming down. Guess we'll just have to surprise her."

Mike got the remainder of the flowers and placed them in Noah's lap and lifted him up – his leg-cast sticking out to the side. Stepping as lightly as possible down the stairs they crept up behind Naomi working at the stove.

"Got a surprise for you," Mike whispered.

Naomi slowly turned with the spatula in her hand. She gave them both a scolding mother look, but couldn't hold it and smiled sweetly.

She leaned in, lightly squeezed Noah's cheeks and kissed him. "No jostling about. I don't want any stitches coming undone."

As they encircled Noah with love something like a magnetic force drew them together. Mike's soul swelled with inspiration. Walking over to the sofa he lowered Noah down and headed to the piano. All he could think of when he sat down were the joyous lyrics to Stevie Wonder's song *Isn't She*

Lovely. Changing the lyrics a bit he burst out singing with all his heart. "Isn't (he) Lovely, Isn't (he) wonderful, Isn't (he) precious…Boy, I'm so happy, we have been Heaven blessed."

Naomi couldn't help herself. She put down the dishtowel, danced in from the kitchen singing and cuddled up to Noah on the couch.

It seemed the minute the sign on the Café door was turned to Open, the phone started to ring. Reporters, agents and well wishers, who had respected the family's time to heal, clambered to get the latest news on Noah and what might be next for composer Mike Monroe. It seemed someone had leaked there was a new composition in the works. Mia was put in charge of taking calls at the Café and dispensed intentionally vague information about the new opus. And the rest of the Y kids returned to their regular jobs of cooking and serving at the Café.

The doctors seemed confident Noah would recover completely from the broken leg, concussion and wounds, but he still needed to be careful for a couple weeks. Mike was eager to keep the kids engaged so scheduled regular practices for the fundraiser. With the Café closed on Mondays, *La Familia* could meet downstairs.

After they had devoured four large pizzas, Mike stood in front of them on the stage in the back corner. "Can't tell you how good it is to see you together again."

Spontaneously, all the kids stood, applauded him and some whistled. Mike straightened, sucked in a huge breath, and grinned.

"Okay…okay," he said motioning for them to sit. "I'm happy to report Noah should be able to be mobile in a couple weeks so I want to get back to practicing for the fundraiser."

Mike had to bite his lip to keep from exploding with what came next.

"As you know, the papers have gone wild following all that has happened with Noah. It appears out of all the tragedy some good has come from it." *Shadow and Light*, Mike thought. "It seems my old music agent has found a new venue for the fundraiser and debut of our composition *Lost and Found*." Mike paused for dramatic effect. "You might have heard of it. The Apollo Theater."

Silence. Mike held out his hands. "Did you hear me?"

Jaz squirmed. "You sure we're ready? Isn't that where pros perform?"

"You guys are pros. You get paid to play here, don't you?"

Jaz snorted. "Don't know if *The Opus* counts."

Mike was disappointed. "Would I get you into something you couldn't handle?"

"Always a first time."

Mike crossed his arms and scanned the group. "Does Jaz speak for the rest of you?"

"Hell no!" Cobi hollered, jumping up from behind his drums.

Slowly, if hesitantly, all but Jaz stood in solidarity.

"Well," Mike said peering down at her. "You with us?"

Jaz slowly stood up. She peered at Mike with her head bowed...and whispered, "Not even my druggy dad played there."

Mike wanted to hug her, but knew it would embarrass her. "He'd be proud of you, Jaz."

47
Lost and Found

After two weeks on crutches Noah was scooting around the Café like a centipede. Mike came in from upstairs to get ready for Monday practice and caught him doing a 360-degree maneuver spinning in a circle on one crutch.

"Hey!" Mike shouted on his way to the piano. "Your mama catches you doing that you'll be back in bed. *Please*...take it easy."

Noah clomped on his crutches over to Mike sitting at the piano bench. "I'll die if I have to go back to bed, Papa."

Mike had to turn away to hide a grin. "Slow down and you won't have to."

When Mike looked back at Noah, he had turned serious. "Papa?"

"Yes, Noah."

"Why do the black kids at school be mean to me?"

Mike squirmed a bit wishing Naomi could be there to help him with this. "I think, Noah, it's because you seem different to them. You're from a different country and talk a little differently." Mike recalled how an old girl friend of his had made a derisive aside about Naomi's dark skin.

"But they different to me, too. I not mean to them."

Mike's heart ached seeing the hurt on his son's face. How could he explain this? "It takes people awhile to understand something new. Adults too, not just kids. You just be good to others."

Mike reached for his son and pulled him onto his lap. "I like that you tell me stuff that bothers you." Mike made a mental note to check with Noah's teachers at school about what was happening there.

Noah gave Mike a quick smile. "Can I play the piano now?"

"You bet." Mike slid the bench out of the way so Noah could stand in front of it with his leg cast. Noah closed his eyes as if seeing something in his mind and started playing a simple melody with one hand. Mike listened, looking back and forth from Noah's hand to his face. When Noah had finished his impromptu composition, he opened his eyes and sighed.

What is this? Mike peered into his son's face. "What's that music about, Noah?"

Noah appeared thoughtful. "It's about watching you in Africa, the bad storm, havin' dinner and livin' with you and Mama."

Mike didn't know if he would laugh or cry. His son was a composer.

$$\text{𝄞}$$

With less than a week before the performance, the kids arrived for practice in their usual state of drama – Mike trying to read the latest crisis from the way they entered the Café. He had learned not to take what he saw *too* seriously. What was high anxiety one minute could change to shrieks of laughter the next. The biggest surprise today, however, was seeing Travis in a state of apparent contrition. According to Naomi, after trying to shake off Mia's affections, the tables had turned. It seemed after a couple weeks of coolness from Mia, Travis discovered he missed the attention. Now it was Mia's turn to play hard to get. Mike recognized the well-worn script from his own experience.

Having not performed at the Apollo himself, Mike had to admit his own growing anxiousness as the fundraiser loomed. He was particularly uneasy that the love triangle of Abby, Blake and Jaz could cause a fracture in the group at any moment. However, after watching Cobi, Tobias, Carlos and Abby enter the Café today, he sensed a totally new dynamic between them – an unexpected joyfulness.

Mike had to find out what was going on as they found their seats on the stage.

"Okay, what's up? You four look like you've just landed a contract with Decca records," he said, pointing to each of them.

Cobi threw his sticks in the air and caught them. "We just got our first gig all by ourselves. Not that we don't appreciate you…Mr. M."

Mike was blindsided. "Gig?"

"Yeah, at the Bottom Line in the Village. We call ourselves *Beauty and the Beasts*. We've put together a dozen songs or so."

"Really?"

"Really. Well…for a night at least. And if they like us, who knows."

Mike raised his eyebrows. "Not sure about the name, but I'm proud of you. As long as it doesn't distract from the Apollo performance."

"We wouldn't do that, Mr. M." Carlos said. "Right?" The others chimed in.

Just then Mike heard Noah shuffle in on his crutches along with his mama.

"Sorry we're late, but this boy needed a nap. Doctor's orders." Naomi said.

Noah took his position with the others – sitting with his recorder in hand and his leg still in a cast. Mike stood a moment and scanned his band of misfits. In a matter of days they would be on stage at the Apollo, Harlem's premier music venue. *Why did this seem so right when so much could go wrong?*

𝄞

Sleep was impossible. Mike lay gazing out at the nightlights of the city with a familiar sense of exhilaration mixed with dread. Naomi rolled over to face him and sighed.

"Sorry. I'm trying to be still," Mike said.

"Are you alright?"

"Why doesn't it get easier with these kids?"

"You wouldn't want that. We don't learn much from things being easy." Naomi was quiet a moment. "You have become their rock, Mike. They are fortunate to have you."

Mike chuckled. "Imagine…me a rock. Who would have guessed?"

Naomi smiled. "Children. They can make you or break you."

Mike caught her smile. She *was* God sent.

49
Now What? – The Opus Café

After the Apollo performance and a raucous party back at the Café, Noah was put to bed and all the band had left but Jaz, who sat at a table with Mike and Naomi – all three lost in thought as they stared out the window.

"Now what?" Jaz asked, turning to Mike.

The sudden quiet and patter of rain outside had put Mike in a reflective mood. He shrugged and cast a look over at Naomi. "What do you think?"

Naomi leaned back in her chair. "I don't want to think about what's next quite yet, because what happened tonight was…amazing."

Mike nodded in agreement. "I was stunned by the comments from some in the reception line afterwards. 'The boy with the cast touched my heart with his playing.' And another, 'The musicians seemed young to be performing at such a high level.' And then there was Leon Kohn. 'Fantastic. I see now your heart lies with these kids. But if you want to use that composition for a musical, I might be interested.' Finally beginning to relax, Mike drew in a long breath. "I couldn't be more proud of every one of them."

Naomi reached for Jaz's hand. "What was your favorite part about tonight?"

Jaz rolled her eyes. "I don't know. Just wish my mom was there. She never comes to hear me."

Mike studied Jaz. "You know she couldn't after getting her new position as shift supervisor."

"Yeah, it means a lot to her."

"She's doing her best, Jaz."

Jaz softened. "I know."

Mike changed the subject. "So, not many people can say Ray Charles showed up to see them. He said he wanted to hear you play when we first met him at Nana's home on Long Island."

Jaz heaved a sigh. "Okay, *that* was pretty cool."

"Yeah. He walked right by me to give you a hug. Guess he thinks you're special."

Jaz seemingly couldn't help herself and broke out in a grin Mike hadn't seen for awhile.

"And don't forget the whole purpose for the fundraiser. The place was packed." Naomi said.

Just then the wall phone behind the counter rang. Mike got up and hustled to answer it, thinking there must be some emergency.

"Opus Café," Mike answered stretching the cord to sit at the counter – quiet as he looked back at Naomi and Jaz.

Shaking his head in disbelief he walked around the counter to hang up.

He stood staring at them. "Not only was it a sell out, seems Brother Ray and Abby's grandma encouraged quite a few of their wealthy friends to contribute extra."

"Fantastic!" Naomi said walking over to Mike. "What did it come to?"

"Unbelievable. Total after expenses is over two hundred and fifty thousand."

Naomi grabbed a stool and sat down.

"Sounds like a lot. Will that build the school?" Jaz said, heading over from the table.

"With some left over," Mike said.

"For books, uniforms and musical instruments," Naomi added.

"Oh, man!" Mike hollered and grabbed Jaz and danced her off into the room. She didn't resist – happily giving in to the celebration.

As the excited trio gathered back at the table with a snack from the kitchen, an aggressive pounding came from the front door of the Café.

Mike went to answer thinking it was probably some guy too drunk to read the sign. "Sorry, we're closed," he yelled, squinting out the rain splattered Café door.

"Got sumpin' for ya," a kid of maybe twelve hollered, holding up a familiar looking backpack.

"What the...?" Mike said, turning the lock to open the door. "Come in, kid."

The scruffy boy walked in dripping wet and looked around the place.

"What do you have there?" Mike asked.

The kid clutched the pack to his chest and held out the other hand – staring at Mike with his jaw set.

Mike's heart raced, eager to see what was left in the pack but couldn't help messing with the kid. "I see. How much for the delivery?" Thinking he'd say at least ten bucks.

The kid lifted the pack as if weighting it and said, "How 'bout...two-bits."

Mike fought back a grin and reached for his wallet. "Because it's a late delivery I think it's worth at least a fin. Is that fair?"

The kid appeared to fight back a grin of his own as he snatched the bill from Mike's hand. "It's pretty heavy," he said holding the pack out to Mike.

When Mike felt the weight of the pack he was really anxious to open it right away but plopped it on the table and motioned for the kid to follow him to the kitchen.

"Would you like to take something with you to eat?"

The kid hunched his shoulders.

Mike laid out slices of bread and piled on salami, cheese and lettuce to make two sandwiches and wrapped them up and put them in a bag along with some chips and a couple of donuts.

After Mike saw the kid out, he sat down next to Jaz and Naomi with the backpack in the middle of the table– all three just staring at it.

Epilogue

"I can't stand it," Jaz said. "Want *me* to open it?"

Mike groaned. "Go ahead. Don't know what I'd do if there's actually money in there."

Jaz pulled the pack in front of her, patted it down like she was trying to guess what was inside, then pulled the zipper down. A bundle of hundred dollar bills slid out with a note tucked in the currency band. Mike picked up the bundle as Jaz lifted the backpack, dumping the reminder of the contents – twenty bundles in all.

Mike slid the note out from the band and read it.

"Saw the reports about your son's ordeal. That was not supposed to happen. I'm very sorry. I've taken a hundred for bus fare but will send it back when I get a job. Hope your boy fully recovers. Regards –"

Mike dropped the note on the pile of hundreds and peered at Naomi in disbelief. He picked up a bundle and fanned it. "This one looks right. Expect the rest will be the same."

"Unbelievable," Naomi said, and put her arm around Mike. "With our money back maybe we should consider the Children's Acting Academy for Noah, after the response from his Apollo debut."

"He's a natural alright," Jaz said.

Mike nodded at Jaz and noticed her fingering Sarah Davis' cross he had given her more than six months ago before leaving for Africa.

"I have to ask, Jaz," Mike said. "When did you start wearing the cross?"

Jaz bowed her head and looked at him from under her eyebrows. "I had to get over being mad at you for leaving."

Mike waited, sensing there was more.

"That and when all the people in the waiting room started praying for Noah...I wanted to be part of that."

As Mike reached around her for a hug, a snicker and a whimper came from the open door to the apartment stairs. All three stood up and held out their arms toward the two smiley faces peering out – one boy and one mutt.

Noah paused a moment scanning them, but before he could move they all ran to him, lifting him up, leg cast and all – smothering him with hugs and kisses.

Noah chortled with joy as Curly ran circles around them.

La Familia de Musica

With the reopening of The Opus, everyone returned to their routine at the Café and other part-time jobs – as much of a routine as is possible for kids on the cusp of adulthood. It seemed Mia had allowed Travis to make amends. The boy, not having a great deal of experience with women, was at a definite disadvantage in the game of courtship and love. *Beauty and the*

Beasts had received lukewarm reviews from the performance at *The Bottom Line* causing Abby to rethink her decision about Julliard. She needed to excel and lukewarm wasn't cutting it for her. After some undercover work by Tobias, through an old girlfriend, Sophia's plan to snare Carlos was exposed. In an explosion of gratitude, after learning Sophia was not pregnant, Carlos had sworn celibacy until he got married. Tobias didn't believe him for a minute. The Beasts part of *Beauty and the Beasts* settled for being the house band at the Café for now – not concerned in the least what might be next for them. Then there was Blake and Jaz. It seemed their collaboration on the R.G. composition kindled a unique relationship that, from the outside, appeared contentious. But, somehow it served something each needed – for Blake someone to stir his soul and for Jaz someone that was completely at ease with the world and could deal with her insecurities – irregular pieces fitting together.

The End

Acknowledgements

Special thanks to my early readers and encouragers: Pam Illies (of course), Zach and Karissa Godel, Sherry Rybak and members of my family. Special thanks to Tiger Hayden-Bracy who, having lived 1980's New York, contributed particulars of the Black experience and Peter Wocken for his awesome design and layout of the book. Dr. Laura Long for insight on medical issues. Then to editors and agents who were indispensable along the way: Laurie Harper, C. S. Lakin, Pamela Illies and Cherry Weiner, but most importantly my wife Janet who's voice and smile frequently appear in the series and who remained encouraging throughout.

Inspiration for the book:

The Opus Series was initially inspired by a disheveled couple I followed into an upscale mall in Minnesota where once inside a smartly dressed shopkeeper sincerely greeted them with a big smile. Having not seen their faces, it struck me I was judging the couple without knowing anything about them. Upon getting home, I told my wife how moved I was by the tender exchange at the mall and thought I wanted to write a story about who the couple might be. She encouraged me then and continues to do so. After seven years, that story has led to three books of the Opus Series. TGTG

About the Author:
Along with the Opus Series, C. Ray Frigard has written two
books on creative problem solving, is a creativity educator,
artist and inventor. He has four grown children and lives with
his wife in Mound Minnesota.

Website:

www.crfrigard.com